THE
CAMERAMAN

Matthew Kneale is the author of eight novels and three works of non-fiction. His debut novel, *Whore Banquets*, won the Somerset Maugham Award; *Sweet Thames* won the John Llewellyn Rhys Prize; and *English Passengers*, shortlisted for the Man Booker Prize and Miles Franklin Award, won the Whitbread Book of the Year Award in 2000. For the last two decades he has lived in Rome with his wife and two children.

Also by Matthew Kneale

THE
CAMERAMAN

MATTHEW
KNEALE

atlantic·*fiction*

First published in hardback in Great Britain in 2023 by Atlantic Books,
an imprint of Atlantic Books Ltd.

This paperback edition published in 2024

1 2 3 4 5 6 7 8 9

A CIP catalogue record for this book is available from the British Library.

Paperback ISBN: 978 1 83895 901 2
EBook ISBN: 978 1 83895 900 5

Printed in Great Britain

Atlantic Books
An Imprint of Atlantic Books Ltd
Ormond House
26–27 Boswell Street
London
WC1N 3JZ

www.atlantic-books.co.uk

To Shannon

One

Julius Sewell's first clue that he might be about to escape came when Orderly Reese made his odd remark. Chilly in his nakedness and his head still bleary from last night's dose of jungle juice, Julius queued for his bath: a gaunt-faced figure with hair that sprouted up from his scalp like blades of ginger grass. The man ahead of him was known for his fear of getting wet. *This'll be noisy*, Julius thought, and sure enough when the other was led forward the air became filled with cries. *Put your fingers in your ears. There – that's better. Have a read of the bath rules.* IN PREPARING A BATH, THE COLD WATER MUST BE TURNED ON FIRST . . . THE BATH KEY IS NEVER TO REMAIN ON THE TAP AND IS NEVER TO BE TRUSTED TO A PATIENT . . .

The shouting stopped, the man re-emerged, still quivering under his towel, and it was Julius' turn to step into the bathroom, with its long row of tubs and their occupants.

I wish they'd fill it a bit higher. It's hardly deep enough to cover my balls. Julius glanced down at the spider of marks on the lower right side of his gut. He could just make out the neat, pale line from his appendix removal, almost lost beneath the other, more recent, purple scars. He reached out with his finger. *I hardly feel them now.*

And that was when Orderly Reese came over. 'Be sure to say hello from me to all the stars, won't you, Pictures? Say hello to Gracie Fields.'

'I will.' By the time the words had sunk in, Orderly Reese had gone. *What did he mean by that?*

His bath over, Julius dried himself and returned to the ward, with its high windows, through which bright sunlight poured. His clothes were waiting on his bed. *This shirt looks all right. And I know these flannels. I wore them just a couple of weeks ago and they fitted me fine. Much better than the pair I had last, which hardly reached down below my knees. See? Today will be a good day.* Then Orderly Reese's words came back, tempting him. *I'm sure he was just making a joke, like all the orderlies do. Though I've told them a dozen times that I never once met Gracie Fields.* Most patients in the Mid-Wales Hospital were from local farms so it was inevitable that Julius, who had worked as a film cameraman in London, would be seen as exotic – hence his nickname, Pictures. *But what Orderly Reese said wasn't really funny. He's the serious one. The other orderlies are always making jokes but not him. And why would he tell me, 'Say hello to all the stars,' when I'm stuck in here?* Feeling a shiver of hope run through him, Julius made an effort to brush it away. *No, I'm not letting you bother me and ruin this day.*

He couldn't ask Reese now, as he and the other night orderlies had finished their shifts and Orderly Evans had taken charge of the ward. *Evans, hell. But he's not that bad. There are worse.* Julius watched him trying to get Tiny Bill out of bed. 'Come on now, you were right as rain just yesterday.' Tiny Bill, a giant boulder of a man, lay quite still, his eyes fixed on the ceiling. 'This is the last time I'm asking you.'

'See, Pictures?' The patient who had a bed two along from Julius, Samson – another joke name, as he was a muscleless stick – threw a glance towards Tiny Bill and then gave Julius a confiding smile to say, aren't we better off than him? 'It'll be treatment for Tiny Bill, I'll bet.'

Julius flinched. *Come on, Tiny Bill, try to get up.* And then he was back to Orderly Reese's odd remark. *But there was something else, too. The look on his face. He had that smile people have when they know something you don't.* Julius shook his head. *Stop thinking about it.* But it was hard.

Orderly Evans gave Tiny Bill a scowl and turned away

– it seemed Samson was right about the treatment – and then began handing out the morning's post.

Sorry, Tiny Bill. 'Unrhyw lythyrau i mi?' Julius asked.

Orderly Evans gave a brief laugh. The orderlies were always amused to hear Julius, one of the few Englishmen in the Mid-Wales, trying to speak Welsh. 'No, Pictures. No letters for you this morning.'

That's more than a week now. Even Lou hasn't written. Julius' sister Louisa normally wrote as regularly as clockwork. *I hope nothing's wrong. I hope you haven't been let down by that Italian fiancé of yours?* He felt a sorrow in the offing. *Everything's fine, remember. You got nice clothes. This'll be a good day.* With rare obedience, the sorrow slipped away.

When everyone was dressed, Orderly Evans bellowed, 'Breakfast,' and, aside from Tiny Bill, who remained motionless in his bed, they began shuffling out of the ward, down the stairs and along a seemingly endless corridor. Patients of another ward were coming the other way and, seeing a wiry man among them, Julius edged towards the wall as far as he could from him, as did others, but the oncomer, talking rapidly to himself, went by without giving any of them so much as a glance.

Another strange thing was that Orderly Reese said it just before he finished his shift, so it was like he was saying goodbye. I suppose he could be leaving? But then he'd have told everyone? And they never leave, as there's no other work in the town, or so everyone says. Julius shook his head. *Go away. Leave me be.*

When they reached the hall, with its smell of decades of brewed tea, Orderly Evans roared, 'Grace,' to sit them down at one of the long tables, and toast, butter, jam and tea were passed down.

Say what you like about this place, the food isn't bad. All fresh from the farm. Julius was buttering his second piece of toast when, from the far end of the hall, there was a quick scraping of chairs and the sound of crockery smashing. Julius and the others at his table jumped to their feet to see. *As I thought – one of the hard cases.* A grey-haired, balding man, his eyes wide with fear, had got another by his neck and was shaking him back and forth. Three orderlies were already running over and soon had him pinned down on the ground. A wild shout rang out, 'Bu'n dweud celwydd wrth y diafol amdanaf!'

'Pictures,' asked the Reverend, who'd been a clergyman in Hay, and knew no Welsh, 'what's he saying?'

'He says the other one was telling lies about him to the Devil.'

The Reverend gave a little nod.

Be glad he was down there, far away from me.

5

'Grace, grace!' came a new roar, to sit them back down.

Samson jabbed his thumb in the direction of the hard case who'd been fighting. 'It'll be the monkey suit for him, I'll bet.' Once again, he was right and an orderly hurried into the hall with the garment, which he and the others set to work pulling onto the man's arms.

And be glad it's not me who's getting the monkey suit this time. The room returned to something like calm. *Orderly Reese is serious normally, true enough, but that doesn't mean he mightn't have been joking just today. He could have a funny side that I've never noticed. And for that matter he did tell me once that he likes Gracie Fields films. Yes, I bet that's the only reason why he said it. Nothing more.* Julius, as he accepted his new explanation, felt his spirits sag, yet also relief, that he was safe now from disappointment. But then, just when he had finally put the matter to rest, a further mystery came to taunt him. Breakfast over, there was a shout of 'Boots', to call him and the others who were fit for work to the shoe room, where Julius picked a laceless pair from the long line on the shelf. He clumped out into bright, mid-March sunshine and set out towards the farm.

Orderly Evans was walking beside him. 'Morning, Pictures.'

'Bore da.' *Another smile for my trying to speak Welsh.*

'First you'll be on the pigs with the Reverend,' said

Orderly Evans. 'And then you'll be weeding the potatoes with Captain Williams. All right?'

'All right.' *See? It's turning out to be a good day, just like I said. You got good clothes. It's sunny and bright. Look at the tiny green leaves on that tree, just beginning to sprout, and the shadows they make on the ground. I had to get a shot of a tree like that in that picture I did about Cornish smugglers, where the director wanted it to look like a gallows shaking in the wind. What was that picture called?* He stopped himself. *You'll be feeding the pigs, which you enjoy, and the Reverend's fine to work with. And though weeding potatoes is hard on the back, Captain Williams is a good sort. You always like spending time with him.* It was then Julius noticed that Orderly Evans, whom he'd assumed would be hurrying on to tell the others their chores, was still beside him.

'Oh, and another thing, Pictures. After lunch I'm to take you to Dr Morrison, as he wants a word.'

At the pigsty, Julius and the Reverend cleaned out the feed trays at the handpump, filled them with kitchen scraps and slid them into place. Usually, Julius liked to watch the pigs eat, snorting with content, but today he hardly saw them. Something was up, of that there was now no question. He was only called to Dr Morrison once a month and he'd last seen him less than a week ago. Why was he being summoned again? Though Julius could no longer crush his bubbling hopes, he tried at least to put them in doubt. *It could be something quite different. Treatment, even. True, I've been much better lately, but that doesn't mean I can be certain.*

After feeding the pigs, Julius spent a couple of hours crouched in the potato field, tearing up weeds, while Captain Williams, who'd been buried alive when his trench collapsed, so everyone said, told him about the plan he was going to send to the top brass. 'This one will take the Huns completely by surprise, Pictures. First we'll launch an attack, all guns blazing, but then we'll fall back like we're in panic, and retreat past our trench and beyond. But when they come after us, we'll have another whole line all ready, stronger than the old one. We'll catch them in an ambush that'll really tear them apart. But don't tell a soul. D'you promise?'

'I promise.'

Lunch was always the best meal of the day, and today was no exception – lamb, potatoes and carrots, with rhubarb and custard for pudding – but Julius hardly tasted a bite. He'd just finished his last spoonful when he saw Orderly Evans walking into the hall. *What if I say the wrong thing? What if I ruin everything?* His anxiousness grew as he walked into Dr Morrison's office. The well-ordered tidiness – the framed medical qualifications and landscape pictures on the walls, the warm-brown carpet, the bookshelf with its neatly arranged books – was so unlike the rest of the hospital that it always made him feel out of place. Orderly Evans retreated discreetly into a corner and Dr Morrison ushered Julius to a seat.

'How are you doing?'

'Fine. I'm quite well, very well in fact, thank you. I'm really absolutely fine.' *Too much – I'm sure that was too much.*

'Everything all right on the ward? At the farm?'

'All fine, thanks.' *He's taking notes.*

'And what about the business that troubled you so much when you first came here? You told me there was a device somewhere in your belly. A kind of little wireless that was giving out signals.'

I knew you'd ask about that. 'I was mistaken, Doctor. I don't think about that any more.' *Hardly ever. Just sometimes.*

'But this device was there before?'

He's trying to trick me. 'No, I was quite wrong about it. It was never ever there.' *Of course it wasn't. I'm almost sure. Or I got it out that time.*

Dr Morrison jotted down a last note. 'Well, I have some good news for you, Julius. Your stepfather telephoned yesterday and asked me if you're ready to leave us and return to life outside this hospital. And I told him that, in my opinion, you are.'

9

For a moment, out of habit, Julius tried to resist the news but then he let go and a dizzying joy spread through him. *It's happening. It's really happening. At last, after all this time. Just when I thought it never would. So I was right about Orderly Reese. He must've heard. What he said about Gracie Fields – that was his way of saying goodbye.*

'What d'you think?'

'It's wonderful news, Dr Morrison. Wonderful.' A counter-wave passed through him as, for the first time, he pondered what this news might mean. *I hope I'll be all right. I hope it doesn't all go bad and they send me back.* He calmed himself. *One thing at a time. All that matters now is that I'll be out of here.*

'Your mother and stepfather will be coming up to collect you tomorrow at noon.'

Julius fought away a feeling of distaste. *Don't think meanly of them. They're coming to take you away from here. Be grateful. Thank you, Mother. Thank you, Claude.*

'It's all very sudden, I know,' said Dr Morrison. 'But I understand from your stepfather that there's a family event coming up, which he and your mother would very much like you to attend. I don't think they'll mind my telling you. One of your sisters is getting married.'

'Louisa?'

'Yes, that's right.'

So you're getting hitched to your Roman, Lou. Good for you. I bet that's the surprise you mentioned in your last letter. Quite a rush. Is it a shotgun wedding? As if it matters. And I'll be there, I'll be there. If they don't change their minds.

But as the hours passed, there was no sign that anybody would. That night, Julius was so excited that as he lay on his bed, snores all around and sometimes a sudden shout, despite his dose of jungle juice he found it hard to sleep. *In just a few hours I'll be gone. I won't be in this dormitory with snorers all around. And tomorrow I'll be sleeping* . . . He found it hard to think of where he might be. *Somewhere else.*

The next morning, he said his goodbyes to the orderlies and patients he was friendly with. Captain Williams gave him a salute. *Does he think I'm going to the war?* Samson seemed in awe of his leaving, and the Reverend, a little mournfully, offered his congratulations. *Don't smile too much. Show that you're sorry that they're still here.*

After breakfast, Julius watched the others shuffle away to the shoe room without him and then Orderly Harris led him away to find a suit. 'Usually with leavers we get the tailors to make something up,' he explained apologetically, 'but there was no time for you, Pictures, more's the pity, as everything was such a rush.' He waited patiently as Julius tried on a dozen jackets. 'There's lovely, eh?' he said, when Julius found one that fitted relatively well. 'So tell me, Pictures, how long have you been here with us now? A year?'

'More like a year and a half.'

'Well, aren't you the lucky one, going away. Most that come in here never do, except when they lay their backs on the mortuary slab.'

Please God, though I don't really believe in you, I beg you, don't ever send me back to this place, nor to anywhere like it. Julius picked a pair of shoes, not the boots he wore when he worked at the farm, but real black shoes with laces, and though they were a little too big so his feet slid about, he smiled at the very sight of them. Proud in his new clothes, he waited in one of the day rooms, watching the patients who were too old or weak or too lost in the head to work on the farm, and who sat blank-faced as the radio played. And then, wonder of wonders, Orderly Harris returned and led him back down the interminable corridor, past the hall, below the clock tower, and into Dr Morrison's office. The doctor, Julius' mother Lilian and his stepfather Claude all turned together as he walked in. *Thank you for coming for me. Mother looks strained. Claude looks annoyed. I'm sorry I never liked you, Claude, really I am. This will be a new start, I promise. Everything will be better between us from now. We'll be great pals.*

Julius' mother stepped towards him but then stopped. 'What's that smell?' Her voice sounded shrill.

'Oh, that'll be paraldehyde,' said Dr Morrison.

Jungle juice. Julius felt a spasm of shame. *I hardly notice it any more.*

'We use it to keep the patients calm,' said Dr Morrison, turning to Julius. 'Did they give you some last night?' Seeing Julius' nod, he frowned. 'I specifically told them not to. But don't you worry, Mrs Reid, as it'll soon work its way through. Another day or two and the odour will be quite gone, I assure you.'

'He smelt like that when we came last time, Pet,' said Julius' stepfather, reaching for her hand to squeeze it. 'You were so upset you probably didn't notice.'

Julius could smell it on himself now, ever more strongly, till he felt he reeked of the stuff.

'A couple of things,' said Dr Morrison, businesslike now. 'It's very important that Julius should avoid all alcohol – wine, spirits, beer, anything at all. I'm not saying that was the cause of his problems, but his drinking won't have helped.'

Claude gave Julius an expectant look.

'Of course,' said Julius. 'I promise I won't touch a drop.'

'Very good,' said Dr Morrison with an approving smile. 'And if you have more strange thoughts or feel troubled,

I want you to tell someone right away. Someone you're close to. One of your family.'

Which? Julius smothered the thought. *They're getting me out of here.*

'I will. I promise.' *Is that it?*

It seemed so. Claude reached out to shake Dr Morrison's hand. 'I want to thank you, Teddy, for keeping such a good eye on him.' Julius' mother cooed agreement. Goodbyes were said.

It's happening. I'm walking out of the waiting room.

'Teddy Morrison's a good man,' said Claude. 'A damn good man. Did I tell you we were at school together?'

You sound angry. Did I say something wrong? 'Mother mentioned it in one of her letters,' said Julius. The detail had stood out, as her correspondence rarely strayed from describing small, everyday occurrences: tea with neighbours, lunch with relatives, or a new watercolour she had finished, of a tree in blossom in the garden or a pretty scene on the river with an old sailing boat.

'He was almost head boy. Should've been, too.'

Here's the main door. And here I am, stepping out into the sunlight. It all seems so easy, so quick. When I woke yesterday morning I had no inkling this might happen, not the slightest idea. Already that seems half an age ago. And look, it's the car! The same old car.

Claude waved to the driver, who was leaning against the door reading the paper and hadn't seen. 'Come on, man, for goodness' sake,' Claude murmured, waving again.

Mother looks so awkward. I should say something, but I can't think what. 'It's been quite a while.'

It was the wrong thing. 'We meant to come up a few weeks ago,' said Lilian, flustered, 'but we wanted to be sure you were ready, and then . . .'

Claude's giving me a scowl. I wasn't complaining, really I wasn't. 'I'm just so glad you came.' *Yes, that's better.*

Lilian gave a little smile, but then the startled look she'd had when she smelt the jungle juice returned. 'What happened to your clothes?'

She thinks this suit's awful. And I thought it was rather good. 'They would've made something up for me but there wasn't time,' Julius explained. *I'm talking too fast. Slow down.* 'So I had to pick it from what there was. Everyone's clothes get mixed up here, you see.'

'He was very oddly dressed when we came up before, remember, Pet?' said Claude, again looking towards the car. 'What does he think he's doing?' He shouted out, 'Sam!'

Sam? Now that he looked more carefully at the driver, who was hurriedly folding away his paper, Julius realized he didn't know him. 'What happened to Toby?'

'We couldn't keep him on,' said Claude. 'You'll find

15

there have been quite a few changes since you . . .' He left the phrase hanging. 'Things got very sticky for the business when the government took the pound off the gold standard. We owed for the wine that we'd already been sent and then the franc went sky-high. I tell you, there were a couple of times when I thought I might go under. Cook had to go, too. Your poor mother's been a perfect saint, making all our meals.'

Her investments must have taken quite a dive.

'I've rather enjoyed it,' said Lilian. 'But it's been awfully difficult for your poor father.'

My stepfather. You always say that. Julius stopped himself. *Don't get annoyed. They came to get you, remember. Think well of them.*

'That's why we had to take you out of Ticehurst,' said Claude. 'When we realized that this was all going to take a good while . . .'

Ticehurst? Julius hadn't even known the name. He had a hazy recollection of heavy wooden furniture, billiard tables and well-kept lawns. He'd had his own room. There had been a patient down the corridor who the orderlies fawned on and addressed as Your Grace.

'And then I remembered that my old pal Teddy Morrison had gone into this . . . this . . .' Again, Claude struggled for the right word, '. . . this line of work. So I did a bit of detective work and found he was up here. I gave him a bell and he said, but of course, Claude, send your boy Julius over right away as a private patient. I'll look after him.'

You're awkward because you sent me somewhere cheap. 'Actually, I think I preferred it here,' Julius said. 'Even though I was on a ward and all the rest. The orderlies are friendlier. And I liked working on the farm.' *Yes – that was the right thing to say. They look relieved. Mother, anyway.*

'Ah, here's Sam,' said Claude.

The car stopped before them and the driver climbed out to open the doors. Julius took his seat in the front. As they began to move off, he watched through the wing mirror as the hospital and the clock tower shrank away and, to his surprise, he felt a sudden urge to call out for them to stop. *Out here everything feels so wide and open. I feel safe in there, in a way. I know everything – which orderlies are kind and which ones aren't, which boots to pick in the shoe room and how to do the farm chores. I know the patients, who to talk to and who to keep well clear of, and how to read faces for trouble.* He closed his eyes for a moment and, as they reached the main road, he felt himself grow calmer. *I'll be all right. I'll be fine.*

'It's already almost half past twelve,' said Claude. 'Perhaps we should catch a bite to eat somewhere nearby before they stop serving. It's a long drive home.'

'There's a place in the town that does lunch,' said Julius. 'It's not bad.'

'Really?'

He can't understand how I know. Julius swivelled round in his seat to face them. 'One of the orderlies would sometimes take a few of us there as a treat.' *Their faces. How stupid of me. Of course, they don't want to go to a place where they might meet people from the hospital.*

'Or there might be a pretty little place along the road,' said his mother, her voice rising again.

'What a nice idea, Pet,' said Claude hurriedly.

Already they had reached Talgarth. Sam the driver stopped at the crossroads. 'I don't suppose you remember which way we drove in, Major?' asked Sam.

Don't ask me. I was in the back of a van when I first arrived, trussed up like a chicken, and I couldn't see a thing.

'Let me see,' said Claude. 'I think it was from over there, wasn't it?'

'Right you are, Major. Yes, that looks like the one.'

They drove out into fields, and then passed down a narrow road with lines of trees to either side, their branches meeting overhead, so it seemed as if they were going through a kind of tunnel, flecked green with tiny spring leaves. Julius glanced up at the foliage speeding by above him – *that would make a good shot* – and felt his spirits rise. *It's so beautiful here.*

And just think, I can go anywhere I want. There's nobody to tell me to sit down or come inside or put on my boots or take my jungle juice. I could go and take a walk on that hill, or sit on that gate for just as long as I like.

The car had fallen into silence. *I should say something.* He had no trouble thinking what. In one of her letters of the previous summer, amid accounts of teas and watercolour paintings, Lilian had mentioned that Julius' half-sister Harriet had married a distant cousin, Harold White. To Julius' surprise, his mother had offered no further details of this momentous news, and though he had asked about it several times in his replies, she had never elaborated. Julius found it hard to believe. *Harriet married. I still think of her as a schoolgirl.* He tried to remember when he had last seen her. *The time when she came to the studios, probably. That must be almost two years ago. People can change a lot in two years.*

Julius had been about to start work on Waltzing in Warsaw, his first chance to shoot a quality, full-budget picture rather than a quota quickie, and, anxious to make a success of it, he had been busy checking the sets and meeting the others who were to work on the film, yet he had found time to give Harriet a tour of the studio. When they passed a well-known screen star he expected her to be impressed, but she'd hardly given him a glance. Afterwards, over lunch in the canteen, she asked Julius a series of questions about how films were made and then had him recount the entire plot of Waltzing in Warsaw, which she disapproved of, complaining that he should have been involved in something more serious. *As if I minded what it was. I was just glad to be working on a big film.*

As to Harriet's new husband, Harold White, Julius hadn't seen him for ten years or more, and he remembered him as an excitable boy. *He was always talking about what he'd be doing next, whether it was next year, in his life ahead, or whether he should ring for a pot of tea. And then something went wrong for him.* Julius tried to remember. *That was it.* Harold had set up a clandestine school magazine in which he wrote caustic comments about the teachers, and when this was discovered, he was expelled. *Harriet and Harold. Harold and Harriet. H and H.* 'And of course Harriet's got married,' Julius said. 'How was that?'

'Dreadful,' said Claude. 'Utterly irresponsible. And so ungrateful to your poor mother.'

How was I to know? That's why Mother wouldn't tell me anything about the wedding in her letters.

Harold and Harriet, Claude explained sourly, had eloped to Mexico together, leaving only a note. 'They wanted to go to Russia, so I heard,' said Claude, 'but they couldn't get a visa. I always thought Harold was a decent chap, but he's turned into the most awful type. A fanatical Red. And he has poor Harriet completely under his spell.'

Julius thought of Harold's subversive school magazine and Harriet's disapproval of Waltzing in Warsaw. *As if Harriet could be under anybody's spell.*

'They wanted to stay on in Mexico,' said Claude, 'but then Harold got ill with a bad stomach, that sort of thing. Now they're in some awful slum in Bermondsey.'

'They're very young,' said Lilian indulgently. 'I'm sure they'll change their ways with time.'

'Let's hope so,' said Claude. 'But . . .' He stopped because Sam had slowed the car.

'Sorry to bother you, Major, but I'm not sure this road looks quite right.'

'Not again,' murmured Julius' mother softly.

Julius felt himself smile. *Claude was always terrible at directions, and now he's found a driver who's just as bad.*

They were approaching a village. 'What about asking her?' said Claude, pointing to a woman who was emerging from her house, carrying a sack of potatoes.

Sam stopped the car beside her and had Julius wind down his window. 'Excuse me, missus,' he said, leaning past Julius, 'but can you tell us the way back to England?'

Julius saw the confused look on her face. *She doesn't understand.* 'Rydum am fynd i Loegr?' he asked.

'Rhaid i mi nôl fy ngŵr,' she answered, smiling now. She put down the sack and went back towards the house, calling out, 'Daffydd?'

'What the hell was that?' demanded Claude.

I should have kept quiet. 'I learned a bit of Welsh in the hospital,' Julius explained apologetically. 'Some of them hardly speak English there.' *And it helped, somehow. I don't know why, but I felt better when I tried to speak another language.* He nodded towards the house. 'She's gone to fetch her husband.'

A moment later the woman re-emerged from the house, now followed by a man who walked with a crutch, his left trouser leg sewn up, empty. 'Yes?' he asked.

'We're lost,' said Sam. 'We're trying to get to Hereford.'

'Well, you're quite wrong up here. You want to go back the way you just came, and then when you get into Talgarth, turn right.'

As Sam thanked him, Claude wound down his window and held out a small silver coin. 'Please take this as a token of our gratitude. I was in France too. We old servicemen have to stick together, eh?'

You were in the Supply Corps. You never saw a trench. Julius stopped himself. *Don't think meanly of him.*

The other man looked at the sixpence for a moment and then slipped it into his pocket. 'Well, ta.'

'A good man,' said Claude as Sam turned the car around. 'A damn good man. I tell you, the ordinary working men of this country are as good as they come. Pure gold. Everything would be fine if it wasn't for these agitators, leading them down the garden path. Take those unemployed marcher chaps we ran into yesterday when we got a little lost. Where was that?'

'Wolverhampton, Major,' said Sam. 'I'm pretty sure it was Wolverhampton.'

'They'd have been right as rain if agitators hadn't got to them.'

'That was so awful,' said Julius' mother. 'They were all shouting and then one spat on the windscreen.'

Julius could imagine the scene: the ragged crowd around the car, angry faces looking in, then one leans close and . . .

'Tom will sort it all out,' said Claude briskly.

'Tom?' asked Julius.

'Mosley, of course,' said Claude. 'Oswald Mosley. To his good friends he's always Tom.'

For a moment Julius tried to make sense of the name. A politician. Julius had never been too interested in politics, while it was rarely discussed in the Mid-Wales Hospital. Religion, yes, that came up all the time. Like the hard case who'd started that trouble at breakfast. *Was that really just yesterday?* 'Mosley's in the Labour Party, isn't he?'

Claude laughed. 'That was yonks ago. He soon saw through that awful shower. He set up his own party, the New Party. You must've heard about it, as that was before you . . . Anyway, then he went the whole hog and now it's the BUF, the British Union of Fascists. I'm in, so is your mother, and Sam here, too. That's how we found you, isn't it, Sam?'

Sam gave a smile of confirmation.

'Of course, I'm just in the women's section,' said Lilian. 'I should really go more often than I do.'

'But you're a paid-up member, Pet, and that's what matters,' said Claude approvingly. 'I'm not full-time, what with running the business, but I do what I can. And I haven't told you this yet, Pet, but I've half a mind to stand at the next election. What would you say to that, eh? Being the wife of an MP. Perhaps even a Cabinet Minister?'

Lilian smiled uneasily. 'Lovely.'

I've been in that place so long that I don't know anything any more. 'Fascists?' Julius said. 'Like Mussolini?'

'That's the ticket,' said Claude. 'But British, of course. British through and through.'

I never much liked Mussolini. All that strutting about in his uniform and shouting. But then what do I know?

Perhaps everyone's in this BUF now? Perhaps I should be, too. Though Claude didn't say I should join. They probably wouldn't want me.

They had reached Talgarth, where Sam turned right at the junction as instructed, and before long they reached Hay-on-Wye. They passed a sign stating that they were entering England and moments later Claude pointed to a pub with a sign outside offering sandwiches. 'What about that little place over there?'

'Perfect,' said Lilian.

Sam stayed in the car and Claude, promising to bring him lunch, led the rest of them into the saloon bar. *How nice it is to see women's faces.* One, sitting at a table across the room, looked familiar. *She reminds me of one of the actresses I did portraits of. Edna Berger, that was her name.* Julius would take stills of actors when they had finished filming for the day, and were still in costume and made-up. If he could convince the art director to leave them switched on, he used the lights on the set. *To try and get my career going and move me up to assistant cameraman. If I got some good shots then they might ask me to do their next film.* Julius recalled his own ambition with a slight sense of wonder, as if it had belonged to somebody else. *And it worked, too, with Edna.*

Plates of musty-looking ham sandwiches had arrived. 'So we'll be setting out on Sunday,' said Claude.

'Setting out for where?'

'Rome, of course.'

Julius had assumed that his sister was getting married in London and for a moment he found the news hard to take in. *I'm going to Italy? Italy, where I've never been?* So many things were happening so quickly that he had a sense of precariousness, as if it might all topple away in an instant. *Yesterday I was pulling up weeds with Captain Williams, without much hope of ever doing anything else, and now I'm going to Italy. What's Italy like?* For a moment his mind went blank. *Pasta and paintings, churches and ruins.*

'I told her, stand your ground, but no, she's doing it all their way, more's the pity,' said Claude grumpily. 'She has a priest who's teaching her all that Catholic mumbo jumbo nonsense. But I suppose you can't have everything, and she's twenty-six now. I mean, thank goodness she's finally found somebody.'

Is twenty-six so old?

'And her chap seems a very good egg. Italian, of course, but a very decent sort. He's something in the government over there.'

'Their home office,' said Lilian. 'Or is it the foreign office?'

'One of them. And he's doing rather well, so I understand.

26

He's always dashing off to meet Mussolini. Frederico di something-or-other, he's called. Quite a mouthful so we all just call him Freddy. We both liked him when they came over at Christmas, didn't we, Pet?'

'Loved him,' said Julius' mother.

Julius felt a faint jab of pain. *You came all the way to England, Lou, and you didn't even write and say, let alone come up and see me? For that matter, you never troubled to tell me that you were getting married.*

'And the wedding's in a darling little church,' said Lilian. 'According to Louisa, it's almost as old as Jesus himself.'

Claude began recounting the plans for the journey. 'I have to say it all worked out rather well. There are some wineries that I've been meaning to visit for a while so I thought, why not motor down and make a trip of it? And it fits in perfectly with your little brother Frank's Easter holidays.'

Little Frank. Julius tried not to let his spirits sag.

'We'll stay a couple of nights in Paris to see Aunt Edith and Uncle Walter.'

More faces Julius hadn't seen for many years. 'I thought they were in India?'

'They moved to Paris a year or so ago, after Walter retired,' said Claude. 'And from there we'll go across to Munich to pick up Maude.'

Claude and Maude. Maude and Claude. I can't believe they never thought of that. So that's where she is – Munich. Julius' half-sister Maude had been even more elusive in her letter-writing than his mother. In all the time Julius had been at the Mid-Wales Hospital she had written only once, and though the letter had been several dozen pages long, each scrawled with her large, slanting script, it had focused wholly on the previous couple of days, so it had been hard for Julius to get an impression of her life. It took him several pages and a glance at the stamp on the envelope to realize that she wasn't in England but somewhere in Germany, where she was studying at a private school run by a woman who was always referred to as 'the darling Baroness'. A sizeable portion of the letter recounted how, the day before, a girl called Millicent had, as a joke, stolen another girl's watch and hidden it under a book, which Maude had considered 'too hilarious'. Much of the rest was taken up with a detailed description of Maude's favourite tea rooms: which cakes she liked best, which ones she didn't like at all, one cake which she had yet to try, as she was saving it for a special day, and how someone called Hitler was so frequent a visitor that he had his own table permanently reserved for him. Maude was always hoping he might ask her over to join him, but he never had. Julius had been puzzled by the name, which was familiar, though he had been unable to remember anything about the man besides a small black moustache.

'Sam will drive us as far as Munich,' Claude continued, 'but after that we'll be too many in the car, what with Maude, so he'll take the train home and I'll drive us on to Italy.' Claude gave a little laugh. 'People will probably think I'm some kind of commercial traveller off on a jaunt with his family.'

That's not really a joke. It's what you really do fear. Once again, Julius told himself off for mean thoughts. 'And Harriet?' he asked. 'I imagine she'll be going?'

'Of course,' said his mother. 'She's taking the train down with Harold.'

'Third class,' said Claude, with a faint snort. 'To be with the workers.'

'But they're stopping in Venice, where we'll meet them for a day or two, which will be lovely,' said Lilian.

Venice? I've always wanted to go there.

'And afterwards we'll drop in on my cousin Ivor in Tuscany,' added Claude.

Another place I'd like to see. Paris is the only one I've been to, and that was years ago, when I was just a boy. I really should have travelled more. But even when I had a little money, I was always worried that I might miss out on a film job. Julius was aware of something puzzling him, and that wouldn't leave him be, like a buzzing fly. 'It sounds like you've been planning this for some time?'

'Absolutely ages,' said Claude importantly. 'You have no idea what a business it is to get something like this organized.'

Julius felt the question in his thoughts, as if he were holding it, wondering. *I can't say nothing. I have to ask.* 'But Dr Morrison told me that it was only yesterday that you rang him to see if I could leave the hospital?'

The table fell into silence. Claude was the one who finally spoke. 'Louisa was so keen you should come,' he said. 'She quite insisted.'

Julius saw his mother give Claude a glance, as if to say, why did you have to say that?

In that one moment everything was suddenly quite clear. *You didn't want me to come. You wouldn't have thought of it, probably, except that Louisa made you agree to bring me.* One realization led to another, which was even worse. *You'd probably have left me in that place if it hadn't been for Lou. It's cheap and far away – the perfect spot to keep an embarrassing family member locked up out of sight.* Julius remembered the letter Louisa had sent, promising a surprise. *That came in the autumn. Is that what happened? You wanted to visit me when you came over at Christmas, Lou, but Claude put you off? Or he and Mother together. They told you that I'd spoil your marriage chances with your Roman, and you gave in? But you stood up to them over the wedding. You insisted they bring me. Claude rang two days ago so all of this has probably only just been agreed. I'll bet there was a hell of a row. And you won. You made them get me out of there. Thank you, Lou.*

'I think it'll be a splendid little jaunt,' said Claude tersely.

Julius glanced at their faces. *We all know that we all know.*

'I'm sure it will,' said Lilian, her voice growing shrill again.

Claude gave Julius a hard look. 'There's something I need to say.'

You're not even ashamed. You almost look pleased.

'We simply can't have any more of this . . . this silliness of yours. This is the most important day of your sister's life and I'm not having you wreck everything and upset your poor mother again. She's been through quite enough as it is. Any more silliness from you, and you'll be straight back in there.' He gestured back down the road to where they'd come from. 'Understand?'

Julius had the oddest feeling, as if his eyes, his nose, his mouth, his whole face were somehow folding into the top of his head.

'Claude, really,' said Lilian.

You say it, Mother, but you say it so quietly. Julius felt he should do something, he should be angry, but it wasn't there inside him. All he found was shame.

The long journey back was driven largely in silence. By the time they reached the outer approaches of London, it was almost dark. Julius looked out at the seemingly endless rows of recently built houses, all but identical, with a bay window to one side, a car parked in front. 'More petrol stations than pubs,' he remembered someone say of this edge-of-London landscape, yet he'd become quite fond of it. *Linda Land*. He'd spent many a day driving back and forth through it on his motorbike, on his way to the studio from whichever digs he'd been living in at the time. He watched a straggle of people getting off a tram, just home from work, and others walking by clutching bags, food for dinner. Lights were switching on in windows, curtains were twitching shut.

'By the way, I almost forgot to tell you, Julius,' said his mother. 'Some producer chap called Simons rang up asking about you.'

Bill Simons. Thanks, Bill. Mother's trying to be friendly. She doesn't want me hating her all the way to Rome. 'Did you tell him where I was?'

'He didn't ask,' said Lilian.

He knew. Of course everyone in the industry will know. And I was just beginning to get somewhere.

'It was just a few weeks ago,' said Lilian.

Julius was surprised. 'Really?'

'And why not?' said Claude. 'In a business like that I'm sure they must be used to all sorts.'

How very ingenious. You manage to scorn me and the whole film world both at once. Julius tried to imagine himself in a studio, full of people, lights blazing. *I'm not ready for that. Not now.*

'Oh, and that girl you used to see rang a couple of times too. Linda. Though that was ages back.'

That was good of her. Thank you, Linda.

They drove along a quiet avenue of large houses, each set well back from the road, and then passed down a brief drive to their own. As a child Julius had resented his step-father moving the family to the house in Kingston, as it had seemed dreary compared to the rambling place where they had lived before, in the countryside beyond Oxford, where you could fish for sticklebacks in the stream, climb trees in the woods, and feed the chickens in the coop, but now he looked at it gladly. *I'll have a room to myself and won't be listening to everyone's snores. I won't have to take any jungle juice.*

'I thought we'd probably get in late so I left some

cold cuts ready,' said Julius' mother as Claude unlocked the front door.

'You're a wonder, Pet.'

'You'll be in the spare room,' Lilian added. 'I had Sarah get it ready. She comes in most mornings. It still feels quite strange, just the two of us here. No cook, no housekeeper, no live-in anybody any more – just us.'

Claude squeezed Lilian's hand. 'But that'll change once business picks up.'

For dinner they sat at the dining table, Claude at one end, Julius at the other and Lilian between them, the radio playing music on the light programme faintly in the background. *Clink, clink, clink of our knives and forks. It's just as well the radio's on, as nobody can think of a word to say. Clink, clink, clink. It's as if all those years never happened.*

To Julius, the room had a scent of old arguments. There had been endless rows during school holidays. Claude and Lilian objected to his developing photographs in the garden shed, which they complained made a smell. Claude complained about Julius' schoolfriends. 'I tell you, the pals you make at school can set you up for life. Your chaps are nice enough in their way, but you need to get to know some fellows who are more, you know, more . . .' *More normal, more English, less foreign – but I suppose I didn't feel very normal, even then.* The Four Musketeers, they had called themselves, in honour of Pierre, though he was actually from Belgium, not France. *And they were good friends.* When Saul heard what happened to Julius, he had visited him twice, first at Ticehurst, then he had travelled all the way out to the Mid-Wales. *A shame he came early on, when I was still in such a poor way. I hardly remember a thing.* He had written many times, as had Pierre and Rajesh, both of whom had returned to their own homes. Rajesh sent long, elegant letters recounting funny stories of his family, of elephants and monkeys. *Trying to make me laugh. And they worked.*

The worst arguments had been when Julius left school and began working full-time for a local wedding photographer, for whom he had done a little summer holiday work. Claude thought this was a dead-end job – *and I suppose it was a little limited* – and wanted Julius to take up an offer to work as a clerk for an old friend of Claude's in the City. *Which was the last thing I wanted to do. And Mother was Bismarck, the dishonest broker, the peacemaker who made no peace, as she always took Claude's side.* The matter had finally been settled when Saul mentioned that his uncle, who ran a film studio, was looking for dogsbodies to help out, explaining that the pay would be bad but it might be quite fun, and that Julius could stay with his family, who lived not far away, till he became settled. Julius had set out shortly afterwards with a suitcase of clothes. *And it went well enough, too, for a good while. Cleaning up in the film room, then clapperboard man, assistant cameraman, first cameraman on three quota quickies and finally on Waltzing in Warsaw.*

After dinner, tired though he was, Julius lay on the spare-room bed for a time, staring absently at a small pottery figurine of a stag on the mantelpiece. He was just dozing off when he heard a sharp clack on the window and, moments later, several clacks together. Opening the curtains, he saw a girl in the garden looking up at him. *Harriet? What are you doing here? And why didn't you just ring the doorbell?* He was about to open the window when she waved at him to stop, put her finger to her lips and pointed towards the front door.

As quietly as he could, Julius made his way back along the corridor, down the stairs and unbolted the door, to find Harriet impatiently looking at him. 'I heard you'd be back today,' she said in a low voice. 'God, you look awful. What did they do to you in that place? You're like a stick. And where on earth did you get those pyjamas? They don't fit you at all.'

You look just the same. The serious schoolgirl. 'They're Claude's. Are you coming in?'

'Better not. I don't want them catching me. And this won't take long. I needed to talk to you alone, as there's no knowing if I'll get a chance when we're all gadding about on the Continent. Now listen, because there's something you absolutely have to do.'

'Oh yes?'

'You have to stop this awful wedding. I'm quite serious. I met Lou's fiancé when they came over before Christmas and he's dreadful. He's a fascist. An absolute brute. A bully. And he has her completely under his spell. I tell you, Julius, you have to free her.'

Julius felt a heaviness descend on him. 'Why me?'

'You're the only one she'll listen to. You two were always like two peas in a pod. She won't take a blind bit of notice of anything I say.'

It's probably true. 'And how exactly am I supposed to break up this marriage?'

'I've seen Pa's schedule for the trip. You'll have several days in Rome before the wedding. Take her aside, get her alone, talk to her. She feels trapped, I know it. I could see it when they came over. All you need to do is make her realize that it's not too late and she'll be out of it all like a shot.'

'But Mother said she adores him. And Claude said this is her last chance, as she's twenty-six. He said if I cause any trouble, he'll send me straight back to the hospital.'

'Pa's a fool, a big fat fool. And of course he loves that ghastly fascist. Don't take any notice of his threats, as you can always hide out with us. You will try, won't you? You have to, Julius, to save your sister. Do you promise?'

'I suppose so.'

'Good man. Now much as I'd like to stay and chat I'd better beetle off, as Harold's waiting in the car. See you in Venice.' She turned and strode purposefully away.

How on earth am I supposed to do this? And what if Harriet's wrong? She and Harold are Reds, so of course they won't like this Freddy. As Julius lay on the bed in the spare room, a sense of despair crept over him, and then a feeling of being still, immensely still, so that all he wanted was to stay motionless and quiet like this forever. Not to move or think. It felt somehow enticing and a clever thing to do. A way to have the world leave him alone. *No, don't let yourself. They'll send you back to the Mid-Wales. You don't want that. Try, try. Think it through. Harriet met Freddy. It can't just be his politics she hates. She saw what he was like.*

Then another thought came to him, giving him a sense of something like purpose. *What if that's the real reason why Lou had Mother and Claude get me out of the Mid-Wales? She wants me to come to Rome so I can help her escape this wedding. She saved me so I can save her. And for all I know Harriet could be right. It might be quite easy.* He was surprised to feel a warming sensation, one that he hadn't had for so long that he had almost forgotten how it felt: a feeling of being needed.

Very well, I'll give it a try. I don't care what Claude says. I'll thwart him. I'll beat him. I'll smash him. He felt a smile break out on his face. *Don't you worry, Lou. I'll come and rescue you from this awful fascist. I'll set you free. It's my promise.*

Two

Sarah the cleaner, red-faced from heaving Lilian's trunk, waved goodbye as the car slipped down the short drive. Claude, as navigator, sat in the front, flapping a map. In the back, Julius was sandwiched between his mother and his half-brother Frank, who Lilian had insisted must have a window seat because of his carsickness.

I don't remember him ever having carsickness. Julius was a little amazed at the quantity of baggage they had. As well as Lilian's trunk, which sat outside on the rack at the back of the vehicle, there was a wall of suitcases stacked up in front of him. Easily the tallest in the family, he shifted his legs to try and be more comfortable, and his knee accidentally touched Frank's, who pulled himself away with a faint, exasperated, 'uh'. *What an awful thought – to be brushed against by your lunatic brother. What if you catch his madness?* Julius found himself wondering. *Could you catch it? Doesn't it run in families? And a couple of Mother's relatives were locked away, poor things. Great-Aunt Mabel and that cousin. What a surprise that would be, Frank, to find yourself in the Mid-Wales, drinking jungle juice and pulling up weeds with Captain Williams. But, no, I'm sure you'll be fine. You take after your pa. More's the pity.*

London was still quiet at this early hour and they passed smoothly through Richmond and Barnes and then along the river. Sam knew the roads and though Claude regularly rustled his map and said, 'Straight on here, Sam,' eliciting a, 'Very good, Major,' there was really no need. Julius peered past Frank, ignoring his half-brother's sour look at this invasion of his eyeline, and he watched the Houses of Parliament drift by across the river. After Tower Bridge they reached an area of poor, low houses, some with boarded-up windows. 'Harriet lives somewhere round here,' said Claude with a shake of his head. 'And Harold's on fifty thousand a year, plus whatever he gets for renting out Wisbury Hall. It's lunacy.'

Julius, who had been looking at a pub sign, caught the word and flinched slightly. *Was that meant for me?*

'They could be in a swanky house in Mayfair if they wanted.'

Not me, he's talking about Harold. He sounds envious.

'Lunacy, lunacy, lunacy,' said Frank.

Claude gave an awkward laugh.

But that was for me, no question. Thank you, Frank. Mother looks like she might say something, but no. Thank you, Ma. Just wait till you all get to Rome and find there's no wedding after all. You won't be smirking then.

They passed the grand facade of the naval hospital in Greenwich and then reached outer London suburbia. *Another Linda Land. Though here the houses look a little smaller. Linda Land East.* As they reached open country-side, Julius pulled out his wallet, still a little puzzled by the sight of money, which was the first he'd had since he'd been taken to Ticehurst. He had gone to the bank just the day before and had been surprised by the amount in his account. Linda must have paid in his earnings for Waltzing in Warsaw. *How very like her. She always did the right thing. Even though she was the one who found me . . .* He shivered slightly. *She still went to the bank for me. Thank you, Linda.*

Julius looked out of the window, past Frank and his mother, at orchards and oast houses. *It's beautiful here.*

After a couple of hours' driving, they passed over a rise in the ground and Julius glimpsed the sea through the windscreen.

'We're almost there,' said Claude. 'Now I should warn you that there'll be times on this trip when I'll have to disappear. I won't say more.' But he then did.

'Tom's given me a few jobs to do. I'd tell all but it's very hush-hush.'

Look at your face, Frank. You love that, don't you? Your father as Bulldog Drummond, the secret agent thwarting the Reds.

'Will you go to see Mussolini?' Frank asked. 'Or Hitler?'

'I wish I could say,' said Claude importantly.

Him again. The one who goes to Maude's tea rooms. 'Who is this Hitler?' he asked.

Frank groaned. 'The president of Germany, of course.'

It's not my fault I didn't hear much news in the Mid-Wales.

'Technically he's not president but chancellor,' said Claude. 'A very dynamic chap. He's only been in charge for a year but he's already done wonders for his country. He's solved the unemployment, which was an absolute disaster over there, and most of all he's saved his people from the Bolsheviks. They were all set to get their claws on the place, which of course would've been a catastrophe for all of Europe.'

I suppose that's good. 'So he's like Mussolini then?' Julius asked.

Frank groaned again. 'Hitler's a Nazi.'

Another name I've heard. 'And Nazis are different from fascists?'

'They're similar,' said Claude.

'Hitler doesn't like the Jews,' said Lilian helpfully.

That again. Saul got enough of it at school. Especially from the first eleven. They were always calling him Yid or Nosy.

'Any sound man will accept that the Jews are a serious matter,' said Claude ponderously. 'And they've been quite a problem for the BUF. Tom was never against them personally, in fact he even has a few Jew chums, or at least he used to, but there was no getting round the fact that a lot of the chaps in the party held pretty strong views. So, sensibly enough, Tom began ramping the party in a Jew-wise sort of way, to keep everybody happy.'

Rajesh they called Blackie or Chicken Curry. Pierre was Frog's Legs, even though he wasn't French but Belgian. And I was Carrot Head.

'But this caused all manner of trouble with the Italians,' Claude continued. 'Because Mussolini, who's helped us out a good deal – all very hush-hush, needless to say – insisted that having a go at the Jews was un-fascist. The upshot is that Tom has to be damn careful. If he's speaking at a small local meeting he can let fly and get the troops fired up, but his official line is that he's only against international finance.' He gave a faint laugh. 'Of course, everybody knows what he really means.'

Though Pierre gave as good as he got. Julius found himself smiling as he remembered how, whenever the first eleven lost a game against another school, Pierre would sing a version of the 'Song of the Toreadors' from Bizet's Carmen. *Two goals to Harrow, none to our poor girls.*

'When it comes to party policy, Tom's come up with a very clever compromise that should keep Mussolini quiet. Unlike Adolf, the BUF won't lump all the Jews together. When we come to power, we'll set up committees of sound men who will interview each and every Jew, then we'll look into their records and see if they're decent patriotic chaps whose hearts are in the right place, or if they're the wrong sort, conniving and international, that sort of thing, and if they're the second lot, naturally they'll have to go.'

And Rajesh called them all after historical figures, which they hated because they had to look them up to see how they'd been insulted. So Tom Brougham, who had such a red, spotty face, was Emperor Domitian.

'Where will they be sent?' asked Frank.

Claude shrugged. 'I don't see that it much matters. It's not as if we're short of places, when we have the whole empire to choose from. Australia, Canada, South Africa and New Zealand might say no, if they go fascist, but that still leaves plenty of other spots. Africa, India, the Caribbean. Palestine, too, though that's a bit of a hot potato.'

Julius thought of the studio boss, Bernstein. *What would he do with himself, boiling away in Bombay or Khartoum?*

'I don't like the Jews,' said Frank simply. 'They wear those odd clothes. They're not like us.'

'I had a Jewish piano teacher when I was young,' said Lilian. 'Miss Epstein. She could be very stern, telling me off when I made a mistake.'

'Poor Pet,' said Claude, turning round in his seat and reaching out for her hand.

'But once I went to see her at a concert, and she played beautifully.'

For a moment the car fell into silence as everybody waited for more, but there was none.

But Saul was the one they went for most, because they could see how much he hated it. Like sharks smelling blood. A little to his own surprise, Julius found he had joined the conversation. 'I don't think I much like the sound of these Nazis.'

Frank let out a groan. 'Trust you to play traitor.'

I'm not a traitor. Though he could not see his face, Julius sensed his stepfather rolling his eyes, Lilian gave a little weary shake of her head and, through the rear-view mirror, Julius glimpsed Sam smirking. *I should say something. But what?* 'The fact is . . .' Julius felt himself grow flustered till he found it hard to remember what they had been discussing. *Damn, damn.* 'I mean . . .' he began.

'Yes?' goaded Frank.

The altercation got no further as the car had reached the port. 'That's the one, Sam,' said Claude, pointing.

They stopped by the ferry and, feeling relief and shame, Julius climbed out of the car into a buffeting wind. Claude sifted through papers in his slim leather case and found a deck ticket. 'We'll see you in France then,' he said cheerily, handing it to Sam, who stayed back to supervise the loading of the car while the family joined a short queue to get aboard. Julius had the sensation that he could feel a vast map extending away from him, stretching interminably onwards, across the Channel, through France and Germany and finally to Italy. He felt a little breathless. *You'll see lots of wonderful places. It may not be as bad as you think.*

It was chance that he was the first on the gangplank. Claude had trouble finding the tickets among the documents in his travelling case, then the papers in his hand flapped wildly in the breeze and threatened to fly away, so he moved behind Julius' back for shelter. 'Damn bloody things. Ah, there they are.' The ticket man gave a nod and waved the four of them on. Julius took a step and that was when he realized. Rather than being solid, like it should have been, he saw that the gangplank just ahead of him was soft like putty. He froze, blocking the others behind him.

'What's going on?' said Claude.

Julius felt rising panic. *I can't just stop here but I can't go on. Should I say something? But Claude won't understand. He'll send me back to the Mid-Wales.* Forcing himself, Julius made his choice. *Anything but to go back there. Be brave like Captain Williams. Sorry, Lou.* Summoning all his determination, he readied himself for the pain he would feel when he scraped against the ship's side, and the shock as he plunged into cold seawater. He raised his foot and felt the balance of his body tip as he stepped forwards, only to find – bafflingly – that he struck hard metal. It seemed almost as if the gangplank had jumped up to meet his shoe. *It's turned solid after all.* Unsure whether to be relieved or disappointed, he walked on, and a moment later they were all standing on the upper deck.

'What the hell was that?' demanded Claude. Frank was smirking and Lilian had closed her eyes.

I saw that it was soft, clear as day. I did. A feeling came over him, one that he had had before and loathed, that everything was slipping about, so he was certain of nothing. *They won't understand.* 'I felt a little faint for a moment.'

'Poor Julius,' said Lilian distantly. 'I hope you're better now.'

When her back was turned, Claude shot him a warning stare.

They stayed to watch as a crane lowered the Austin onto the car deck and then made their way into the smoke-filled lounge. Frank read a schoolbook, Lilian a novel, Claude studied a map of France and jotted in his notebook, while Julius peered out of the porthole at the grey waves outside. When they were well out of port, Claude said he needed to go to the lavatory and, watching him sway out of the room, Julius felt sudden panic. *What if he's going to have them radio ahead so there'll be a van waiting for me? When we get there, should I run? But I don't even have my passport, as he's got it in that leather case. And if I had it, where would I go? Back to England? To Harriet and Harold? I don't even know where they live. And they'll be leaving soon. For all I know, they may already have left.* But though his heart raced as they got off the boat at Calais, and he glanced uneasily at every official, nobody sprang out to seize him. *Perhaps Claude's scared of arriving at Lou's wedding without me? Or he's just waiting his moment?*

The car was craned from the car deck, they were rejoined by Sam, his hair wild from his spell on the deck, and then they moved on to French customs, where Claude showed his travelling pass, AA membership and the triptyque for the car. *The customs man looks amazed. I wonder what Claude said to him? No, it's all right, it's just his French.* Though Julius had only learned the language at school, he knew it well enough to hear how strange Claude sounded. *He's very fluent yet it doesn't seem like French at all, but like English with a very peculiar vocabulary. 'Marchand' is like 'march and' and 'vin' rhymes with 'sin'. No wonder the customs man looks amazed.*

Released at last, they got into the car and set out towards Paris. Twice they took the wrong road and twice the thermostat dial on the front bonnet went to boiling and they had to stop by the roadside to let the radiator cool. Then, when they reached the city outskirts, they became stuck in a long queue to pay the city tax on the petrol in the tank. 'Absurd system,' growled Claude.

'We're going to be awfully late,' said Lilian impatiently. 'We should have taken an earlier boat.'

'I suppose we should have,' said Claude. 'Sorry, Pet.'

Mother has the money. Mother's always right.

Finally they paid their dues and drove down streets of suburban villas. *French Linda Land. But the houses aren't like London – here they're all different from one another.* When they reached the centre and began passing through wide streets flanked with the city's distinctive high, pale-grey apartment blocks, Julius felt the oddest sensation: an intense, troubled excitement, and an urge to cry, for no reason he could understand. *Is it happening again?* He remembered Dr Morrison's advice. *Tell them? I'm damn well not going to do that. If I say one word to Claude he'll send me straight back. Does it show on my face?* Julius cast quick glances at

Frank and his mother. *Thank goodness it's dark*. He tried to settle himself by thinking of his last visit to Paris, all those years ago, only to find this made matters worse. *I can't remember a thing. Not a single thing. I'm sure I could before. It's like it's all vanished. What on earth's going on?*

Rather to his relief, they became lost several times, leading to much flapping of Claude's map, and by the time they finally reached Aunt Edith's flat he felt calmer.

'It's almost nine,' said Lilian impatiently. 'Come on, Julius, for goodness' sake, don't dawdle.'

Why me? I can't get out till you have. Then everyone was standing on the pavement, listening to a din of klaxons as their car was blocking the traffic and other vehicles struggled to get by. Sam ignored the rage of the other drivers and set to work heaving the suitcases, Aunt Edith and Walter emerged from the building, and Lilian apologized for their lateness and offered greetings both at once. 'And here's Julius who you can't have seen for . . .'

'Twelve years,' said Aunt Edith briskly. 'When we were over on leave. You have grown tall, Julius.'

Walter looks like he half expects me to start foaming at the mouth. Do I look that bad? Or is it just because of what he knows about me?

Sam had finally finished with the luggage. 'I'll find somewhere for the car.'

'Good luck in this town,' said Claude.

The lift was small so they had to go in two groups. Julius found himself walking into a flat decorated with Indian paintings. 'Claude, Lilian and Frank, you'll be in the spare room,' said Aunt Edith. 'And you, Julius, will be on a camp bed in the sitting room.' *Same pecking order here. Not that I'd want to be with them.*

Everyone hurriedly changed and then made their way to the dining room. Taking his place, Julius glanced into a bowl of soup. *How tiny the mushrooms are. Will they expect me to join in their chatter? I hope not.* But nobody did. Julius, at the centre of the table, was pleased to find himself ignored by the separate conversations that grew up at either end. To his left, Aunt Edith was animatedly telling her sister Lilian about somebody who lived in a small town in Bengal, and who had married a gorgeous bride, only to ignore her and spend all his days going off to play polo, so she hardly saw him. *Of course, now I see, it's not anyone she knows – it's her new novel. Mother looks strained. I suppose it doesn't feel fair. Aunt Edith sells books by the thousand and nobody's ever asked to buy one of Mother's paintings.* He took a last spoonful of soup. *Did we go up the Eiffel Tower? Doesn't everybody do that?* But there was nothing, nothing at all.

At the other end of the table, Walter was complaining that nobody in England understood India. 'I'd like to chuck every one of those damned do-gooders into the middle of a crowd of Calcutta rioters. That would soon change their tune. I'm not saying that he didn't go a little too far at Amritsar, but in India you have to nip things in the bud and rule with a firm hand or you're lost. The white man has to show he's in charge.'

Claude nodded. 'Quite so.'

Amritsar? Oh God. The massacre had happened when Julius was still at school. *Rajesh wouldn't talk to anyone English, not even me. I told him that I thought it was monstrous, too, but he just said, 'I'm sorry but I just can't.' Till one day he was smiling and chatty as if nothing had happened.*

Walter was reaching towards him with a bottle. 'Drop of Chablis?'

'No. The doctor said I shouldn't.'

'Doctors? A lot of quacks. One little glass won't do you any harm.'

Julius glanced round for help but Claude seemed uninterested and Lilian was too busy listening to her sister, and then it was too late, as Walter was pouring. He gave Julius an expectant look. *It'll look rude if I don't.* Julius raised the glass to his mouth and found, rather to his relief, that it tasted sour and chemical.

'How is it?'

'Very good.' *If I leave it full then he can't give me any*

more. A plate of fish appeared before Julius and, as he tried to remove the tiny bones, he found his hands were trembling.

'And this shower of a government wants to give it all away,' Walter went on bitterly. 'As if the Indians could ever run the show themselves. I tell you, if we up sticks and leave, within three days the trains will stop, the taps will run dry, the bazaars will be empty with not a bite to eat, and there'll be fighting in every street from Calcutta to Bombay. The country will be right back to how it was when we first came in and straightened everything out. It'll be chaos, corruption, violence and barbarism, till the Russians march in and finish the job.'

Julius tried to imagine a world without water or food to buy. *They'd be all right at the Mid-Wales, as they have their own farm. And Orderly Evans said the water comes from a spring.* He frowned. *Museums – did we go to museums? Or art galleries? We must have? Did we visit people we knew here? No, there's nothing.*

Chocolate cake arrived.

'The only one who's really on our side and wants to stop the rot is Winston,' said Walter.

Winston?

'He'd rather see the place go up in flames than give it all away. But of course he's stuck on the back benches.'

'Tom had high hopes that he'd come and join us,' said Claude.

Now I remember. Julius thought of a round, jowly face.

'Just imagine it, the two greatest speakers in the land, Mosley and Churchill, standing side by side,' Claude continued. 'But Winston's too much of a stick-in-the-mud, more's the pity. He can't see that it's time to leave the old gang behind and move ahead to something new.' He broke into a smile. 'You know what, Walter, you should join us. We need chaps like you. And it would be handy to have a man on the ground here to liaise with our French friends.'

We must've gone out to restaurants?

Walter shook his head. 'I'm like Winston, I'm afraid. Too much of a stick-in-the-mud.'

The maid brought a tray of small white cups and then, to his own great surprise, smelling the aroma of strong coffee and hot milk, and seeing the silver pots that were placed on the table, Julius felt as if curtains had been swished open and he was back in a hotel breakfast room. Before him were a cup of hot chocolate and a croissant with butter and dark-red jam, and everything tasted wonderful. *Now I remember. The underground had a strange sweetish smell. And we climbed up a high tower with strange stone creatures that scowled out over the city. Mother bought Lou a little toy cat and I got a dog. But why does it all feel so sad?*

55

Their coffee finished, the others were getting up from their places, and Julius was about to do the same when Walter stopped him. 'Not permitted, old chap. You've still got a full glass.'

I suppose I'm not in a hurry to be on that camp bed, trying to sleep. Julius sat down again.

'I'll have a last one just to keep you company,' said Walter, generously filling his own glass, and he leaned towards Julius with a conspiratorial, toothy smile. 'I know what you need to sort you out. A pretty little bedmate. I bet you've never even had one. In England you can't get anywhere unless you put a ring on her finger.'

We were on a train – going back home I imagine – and something happened, something bad. Why can't I remember?

'You should go to India,' said Walter, emptying his glass. 'No end of chances out there. Plenty of dusky maidens in need of a rupee or two. Or anything else, for that matter.' He picked up the wine bottle but found it was empty. 'What d'you say to a small whisky?' he asked hopefully. 'A chota peg?'

Of course, she'll know. 'No thanks,' said Julius, getting up. 'I think I'd better turn in.' But instead of going to his camp bed, he knocked on the door of the spare room, where he found Claude and Lilian in separate beds and Frank on a camp bed, all three glancing up at him from their books.

'What's going on?' asked Claude suspiciously.

'Mother, I wanted to ask you about when we all came here years ago. When I was just a boy.' *Look at their faces. Claude and Frank never like it when we talk about the time before them.* 'Did something bad happen?'

Lilian looked put out. 'Not at all, we had a lovely holiday. The weather was delightful.'

'But something happened on the train, I'm sure it did.'

Lilian frowned, trying to remember. 'There was some business at the station when we were about to leave. Oh yes, that was it. You were always running about then, you couldn't keep still, you were playing tag with Lou and then one of the railwaymen said we should keep control of you as you might push somebody onto the tracks. He made quite a fuss and your father got rather annoyed.'

Is that all? 'Nothing else?'

'Not that I remember. As I said, it was a delightful holiday.'

Claude looked disapprovingly over his book. 'I'd say the railway chappie had a fair point. I mean, you can't have a little brat scampering round in a busy place like that.'

Lying down on his camp bed, Julius tried to understand. *I suppose that was what was unbearable on the train. Father was angry with me. But why would that make me feel sad now?* Then he remembered. The holiday in Paris had been a special treat for Julius. *Before I went to my first boarding school. I must have gone right after we got back.* And then, that same term, the school secretary had called him out of a history lesson and he had known, that same second, from his face, that something was terribly wrong. He'd sat in the headmaster's study, yellow autumn leaves outside the window, pictures of soldiers in old uniforms on the walls, dreading what it would be, and at first he hadn't understood, and he'd almost wanted to laugh. A stroke? He imagined somebody petting his father like a kitten.

And that was when everything changed. At first it was terrible but it was a little nice too, or so it seemed afterwards, because it was just the three of us, Mother, Lou and me, and we were all in the house in Oxfordshire, at least in the holidays. The war began, the younger teachers vanished one by one to join up, and on a drizzly autumn day Julius felt a sudden, sharp pain on the right side of his belly. He was taken to a hospital near the school where, when he came to after the operation to remove his appendix, a friendly nurse told him that in peacetime he would have been given ice cream. *And then Mother came to visit with a stranger, whose smile I didn't like, and he asked me, 'So how are you doing, little man?' Mother said his name was Claude, and I wondered why on earth she'd brought him there.*

Julius listened to the faint sound of car horns outside

the window. *Perhaps it's a good thing I've thought of all these things? Perhaps it'll be like when chaps like Freud get people to lie down on a couch and ask them questions – except that I've asked the questions myself. Perhaps everything will be better now?*

But when he woke the next morning, he found his spirits had not risen but fallen. Walking into the dining room he found the others already having breakfast. Sunlight was streaming through the trees outside, and the tablecloth was patterned with shadows of leaves, moving in the wind. *Could I shoot that in a studio? It'd be hard. I could have someone wave branches in front of a studio light, but it wouldn't look quite the same.* He shooed the thought away. *As if I need to worry about that now.*

Everyone had plans for the morning. Walter had a doctor's appointment, Aunt Edith was going to the hairdresser, Lilian was having lunch with an old school friend who was living in Paris, and Claude was going on the first of his promised hush-hush errands. 'I thought I'd take Frank along,' he said, 'as he might find it interesting.'

'Let me guess,' said Walter with a laugh. 'The Action Française fellows?'

Claude pulled a face of exaggerated denial. 'I can't say a word.'

'You should take Julius, too,' said Lilian.

Frank doesn't like that at all.

'I'm not sure it's a good idea,' said Claude. 'It's a delicate sort of thing.'

You can't risk having the family lunatic spoil your meeting with French fascists. Julius knew he shouldn't care, as he had no wish to go, but his mood lowered again.

'He could join you and Diedre,' Claude proposed.

'I haven't seen her for so long, we'll be talking old times,' said Lilian. 'I'm afraid it would be very dull for him.'

Or ruining your tête-à-tête lunch. 'I'd quite like to take a walk round the city,' said Julius. *Anything to get out of here. Of course they're not keen on that either. Perish the thought of the madman roaming about by himself.*

'I'm not sure . . .' Claude began, but then Aunt Edith interrupted.

'Why shouldn't he go for a walk?' she said briskly. 'Come to think of it, Julius, I have something for you.' She left the room and returned with a small black box and a bag. 'I got it years ago, I've never used it once and I know I never will, so you should have it. You can take some pictures of the wedding. There are some films in the bag.'

A box Brownie. Like the one I had when I was a teenager. Mine was metal, not cardboard. And the Leica I got later was ten times better. But why not, I suppose? She means it kindly.

'Well, thank you.'

60

Julius took the camera with him when he set out walking, the bag slung over his shoulder. *Here I am, strolling through Paris.* He could hear the words in his head but he couldn't feel them, so it was like chewing something delicious with no sense of taste. *How on earth am I supposed to break up Lou's wedding? I mean, how d'you do something like that?* The camera bag felt heavy on his shoulder. Reaching the river, he noticed how the apartment buildings formed into a curious pattern of greys. *I suppose I should take a picture.* But rather than exciting him, the thought had a heaviness. A clarity came to him. *Don't fool yourself. You know exactly how this will all go. Remember what happened on the gangplank yesterday. You'll never be free of it. Even if you get to Rome, even if you manage to stop Lou's wedding, which I can't believe you will, it'll all go wrong again, as it's bound to, and then Claude will be only too happy to send you back to the Mid-Wales. And this time there'll be no getting out. It'll be like Orderly Harris said, and the only way out will be on the mortuary slab.*

He stopped halfway across a bridge. *That man's looking at me as he goes by. Can he tell? Now he's gone on.* Leaning against the parapet he peered down at the water. *It looks almost still, like brown glass, but it must be flowing quite fast. I wonder if it goes faster where it's stiller?* He took the Brownie from the bag and put it on the stone before him. *I wonder*

61

how cold it is. The air's cold enough, so the water must be. With one finger, he nudged the camera closer to the edge. *If it falls in, should I get it?* He pushed it another quarter-inch, then another, till it was half over the edge. But then, for no reason he knew, he found he had pulled it back, put it in its bag, and he walked on towards the other shore.

He reached a large park where he sat on a bench overlooking a pond with a fountain. *That man, walking with the crutch, he must've been in the war.* An odd thought came to him. *I bet he sits down. At that bench over there.* The man stood for a moment, peering out towards the pond, where several model boats were sailing, then he slowly made his way towards the same bench that Julius had picked out, and sat. *I was right.* Inside himself Julius felt a stirring of something, a faint interest.

What else can I guess? No – that's enough for now. Looking down, he saw the bag on his lap. *Why not?* He took out the camera, opened the back and loaded a film. *But he has his face half turned away. And what if he sees? The pond's better. The people on the far side make an interesting pattern.* For some reason his mind turned to Orderly Reese, Captain Williams and the Reverend. *I wonder what they'd think if they could be here and see all of this? And Linda, too? I wonder what she's doing this very moment? Something good, I hope.* He got to his feet and peered down into the viewfinder. *No light meter, but I can guess.* He adjusted the shutter speed to medium, held his breath and heard the reassuring click. *Perhaps everything will be all right after all. Don't worry, Lou, I'll be there. Probably. If I can.* He put the camera back in the bag. *Will I be able to save her? No, don't ask that. Not now.* And on he walked.

Three

Early the next morning they set out eastwards from Paris and within a few hours they were driving through gently rolling countryside. *How many people will be in the next car coming the other way?* Julius closed his eyes for a moment. *Two.* He watched intently through the windscreen till a car came speeding towards them with two figures seated in the front and none in the back, and a feeling of triumph spread through him. *Yes! Hurrah! Right again.*

They passed several buildings that had been reduced to ruined walls. 'The front must've been round here,' said Claude.

What colour will the next car be? Julius closed his eyes. *Black.* A blue car sped by. *That didn't count, as I knew it wouldn't work that time.* In the distance Julius glimpsed row after row of neat white crosses. *A war cemetery. Will Claude have us stop?* He closed his eyes. *He will.*

'Pull over here will you, Sam,' said Claude as they drew near.

'Righty-ho, Major,' said Sam.

Yes!

As they all climbed out of the car, Julius saw, some distance away, a lanky figure in boots and shorts and a floppy, brimmed hat, who was walking along the roadside towards them, tapping the ground with a sturdy-looking stick. *Odd-looking bird. He doesn't seem like a farmer. Some kind of hiker, probably. Will he wave to us?* Julius closed his eyes. *He will.* From the corner of his eye he saw a slow movement. *Oh hell, Claude's saluting.* Sure enough, Julius' stepfather, facing the crosses, was standing stiffly to attention, his hand raised to his brow. Sam followed suit and then Frank, squinting and squeezing his lips tight shut to show his intensity. *Sam's the only one who's doing it properly. Do I have to, too?* Even Lilian was saluting now, though her hand was too far over, so it looked as if she were trying to get something out of her eye. *I can't very well not.* As Julius raised his hand, he thought of Captain Williams. *I wonder if some of your comrades are here? It's not very likely, I suppose.* Crows cawed. It was such a peaceful place that it was hard to think of what lay below the crosses, and what had brought them there.

'Major?' said Sam tentatively. 'Just to say, but I think this one's Frenchies.'

Glancing round, Julius saw a tricolour flying amid some

trees. Claude gave an awkward laugh and lowered his hand. 'Silly of me.'

So we shouldn't be saluting our gallant allies?

'We'd best press on,' said Claude briskly. 'Lots to do today.'

The walker in the brimmed hat had reached them. 'Sorry to bother you,' he said, 'but I heard you speaking English. I wondered if you could point me towards Chalons? I'm a little lost.'

He raised his hand a bit, which is like waving. Come to think of it, talking is a kind of waving too, but better.

Claude gave the stranger a benign smile. 'Let me guess. You're trying to find fallen comrades?'

'Actually, no,' he answered. 'I'm on a pilgrimage. I'm walking to Rome.'

Claude's face grew distant. 'Sam, can you get the map out from the car?'

You liked him before. Why have you changed your mind? Because he's a Catholic? If he is. Because Lou's converting? Or because you were wrong thinking that he was here for the war cemeteries? Because he wasn't what you'd decided he was?

Driving on, they visited three vineyards. Julius had always imagined Claude's wine tours were romantic, with inspections of cool, ancient cellars and then relaxed lunches, but this wasn't the case at all. At each winery they followed Claude into the tasting room, where he was greeted, sat down, brought a sample of wine, poured roughly into a glass, which he examined, holding it up to the light and inhaling the aroma, before he took a mouthful, frowned, spat into a basin, asked the price and jotted a comment in his notebook. When a number of wines had been tasted in this way, hands were shaken, brief goodbyes said and on they went.

'The Cabernet wasn't bad,' Claude declared, when they drove on from the last of the visits, 'but they didn't seem at all organized. No, I don't think I'll be buying from them.'

Because you saw one of them was biting his lip trying not to laugh at your French? Yet, for all his dislike of his stepfather, Julius was impressed by his professionalism. *I wish I could be like that, and know how to do something difficult – know it really well.* Then he remembered. *I suppose I did, as first cameraman.*

They drove eastwards, passing a whole series of war cemeteries, and beyond Metz they stopped for the night at a small hotel where Claude was convinced that he'd been overcharged for the dinner. 'The waiter asked me, clear as day, would you like a cognac?' he complained, as they set out onto the road the next morning. 'Naturally I assumed it was on the house. What else would he have meant?'

It doesn't follow that it would be free. And it wasn't you who paid. I saw Mother at the reception desk settling the bill.

But then Frank added, 'My soup was cold,' Claude gave a flap of his map and said, 'Awful damn place,' and the matter was decided.

After an hour's driving they pulled in at a filling station. 'Looks like some of our fellow countrymen, Major,' said Sam as he stopped the car at the pump and the attendant began filling the tank. Sure enough, parked nearby were a car and caravan with GB plates. Watched by his wife and two small daughters, a man was clinging to the roof of the caravan, one foot in an open window, as he reached up to retrieve a pennant. Climbing down, he glanced in the direction of Claude and Lilian's car and then glanced again.

He's seen our British plates. Will he come over and talk to us? Julius closed his eyes. *He will.*

'Why are you shutting your eyes like that?' said Frank. 'He keeps doing it.'

Claude glanced back suspiciously from the front seat. 'Is something going on?'

It's none of their business. As if they could understand. It's my secret thing. My gift. 'It's bright today,' he said. 'The sun was in my eyes.'

The caravan owner was walking towards them, his family following behind him.

Yes!

'Nice car,' he said tentatively.

He's wondering if Claude will snub him. And so you should.
'It's pretty comfortable on the road.'

Claude's smiling but not getting out. Like a feudal lord receiving peasants from his throne.

'I'm sure it is.' Seeing them looking at the pennant in his hand, the caravan owner gave it a little wave. 'I thought I'd better get rid of this, as it mightn't go down too well in France.'

I've seen that funny sloping cross before. 'What is that?' Julius murmured.

'A swastika, of course,' said Frank scornfully. 'The Nazis' flag.'

I wonder if it'll work if I just blink my eyes? They probably won't notice that.

'We're on our way to Germany now,' said Claude. 'Did you have an enjoyable trip?'

'Wonderful,' answered the caravan owner dreamily. 'Couldn't have been better. Though you have to steer clear of politics, as they're all mad about Hitler.'

Him again. Maude's tea-drinker.

'Not all of them,' his wife corrected him. 'There was that man in the antique shop. And the one who came up to talk to us in the museum.'

'Most of them,' her husband conceded.

Will Claude give me another lecture on how I mustn't get

up to any more silliness? Julius blinked his eyes and was happy to find nobody noticed. *He will.*

'And it's all so cheap,' said the caravan owner. 'We ate very well. Too well, actually.' He gave his stomach a little slap. 'And everything's spotless everywhere you go.'

Spotless and cheap. Wonderful country, wonderful Nazis. This man's getting a little annoying.

'Except that place where we had the sausages,' said his wife. 'That wasn't clean at all.'

What will happen today? Something very good? Julius blinked. *It will. And something bad, too.* He blinked again. *No.*

'Apart from that sausage place, yes. But everyone's terribly friendly. The moment they saw our GB sticker they were all smiles and they'd come up and tell us that they don't like the French but they love the English.'

Will she say he's wrong again? Julius blinked as the question formed in his head. *She will.*

'Though there was that man who didn't like the English at all. The one who went on about the time after the war, when the Tommies stayed in nice hotels and got drunk at the Germans' expense and the Germans had nothing to eat.'

Yes!

The caravan owner gave Claude a conspiratorial roll of his eyes. 'Yes, aside from him.'

The older daughter held up a toy tabby cat. 'And they have nice toys.'

'Very nice,' said her sister, holding her cat higher.

'Charming family,' said Claude as they pulled away from the filling station.

The way you say it, you manage to praise them and scorn them both at the same time.

They passed a sign that read FRONTIÈRE ALLEMAGNE and Claude twisted round in his seat. 'You heard what that chap said? I don't want to hear anyone saying anything disrespectful about Germany, or Hitler, or the Nazis. Is that clear?'

He's not looking at Frank or Mother, just me. Does that count?

'And needless to say, we can't have any . . .' He hesitated. 'Any silliness of any kind.'

Yes! As if you have to worry about me. I'm right as rain now, you . . . Julius tried to remember what Harriet had called Claude. *You big fat fool.*

At the French frontier post they had their passports stamped, and the triptyque for the car, and then they drove on to the German side where a uniformed official raised his right arm and greeted them with a brisk, 'Heil Hitler.'

'Oh quite so,' said Claude, raising his arm. 'Heil Hitler,' and then Sam, Frank and Lilian did the same.

Do I have to? I'm in the middle so my hand would hit the roof.

Having taken their passports, the official peered into the car to check their faces.

Will he say it again? Julius blinked. *He will.*

Sure enough, satisfied that everyone matched their passport pictures, the border official returned the passports to Claude with another 'Heil Hitler.'

Actually I'm not sure they count. They're too easy.

'Julius isn't saluting,' complained Frank as they drove the few yards to the customs.

Snitch.

Claude turned round in his seat. 'It's a matter of showing respect.'

All right, all right, if it'll keep you all quiet. As they climbed out of the car to have their luggage checked, Julius joined the rest of the family in the chant, though his Roman salute was slow and not very straight, earning him a glance from his stepfather.

'It's not hail Hitler,' sneered Frank as they climbed back into the car. 'It's heil Hitler.'

'My dear,' said Lilian, 'you were thinking Mother Mary.' Everyone was laughing.

How was I to know? Nobody said it in the Mid-Wales.

As they drove on from the frontier post, Frank raised his

arm into the air once again. 'Hail Mosley,' he said.

'Why not?' said Claude, raising his arm. 'Hail Mosley,' and they both laughed a little self-consciously.

'Dad,' asked Frank, 'd'you think I can put on my BUF pin?'

'Damn good idea!' said Claude approvingly. 'I'll do the same. What d'you say, Sam?'

'Mine's in my luggage, Major,' said Sam, 'but I'll make sure to get it out when we stop next.'

Will Mother get out hers? Julius blinked. *Yes.*

'Oh dear,' said Lilian. 'I have a feeling I left mine in Kingston. I had it in my dressing-table drawer. I'm awfully sorry.'

Damn. How did that happen?

'Don't worry, Pet,' said Claude, twisting round in his seat so he could take her hand. 'Three of us will be more than enough to do the party proud.'

The next car will be black. Julius closed his eyes and peered intensely through the windscreen only to see a grey car speed by. *Damn again.* He frowned, concentrating. *The next car will have two people in it.* But instead, it was crammed with passengers and had cases tied to the roof. *Ugh.*

'Claude,' asked Lilian, 'd'you think there's somewhere we might be able to stop? I need to . . .'

73

'Of course, Pet. Don't worry, as we're almost at the next vineyard.'

Claude's skills at navigation, though, which had held up tolerably well in France, now deserted him, and when they passed the next road sign he flapped his map. 'How the hell did we get here? Sam, I'm afraid we need to turn round. And then we should take a left.'

'Righty-ho, Major.'

Julius glanced at a field filled with cows. *The next animal I see will be a cow.* Hardly had he blinked his eyes when they rounded a corner and came into sight of a field with two horses. He adjusted his legs. *There's no room in this damn car. I just don't fit at all. Mother keeps bashing me with her elbow as she does her knitting. And it's so stifling in here.*

They passed a sign with the name of a town and a church spire came into sight ahead. 'Perhaps there might be somewhere here?' asked Lilian, her voice sounding a little shrill.

'Of course, Pet,' said Claude. 'Next place you see, Sam.'

As they entered the outskirts of the town, Julius was puzzled to hear, above the drone of the car engine, a tinkle of music and a radio-like voice that was answered with a cheer. *Some kind of concert?* When they rounded a corner, the road ahead was blocked by the rear of a procession of marchers in leather costumes, holding up colourful banners.

Those swastika things again. Shorts on a day like this. They must have cold knees. Women and children, also in traditional costumes, were standing by the sides of the road, cheering and waving.

'I can turn round, Major,' offered Sam, glancing up at the rear mirror. 'No, there's another car right behind us, and another behind him.'

'That looks like a bar,' said Lilian, pointing and then hurriedly opening the door. 'I rather think I might get out here.'

'Of course, Pet.'

'And me, too,' said Julius suddenly, catching himself a little by surprise. 'I'd like to get some water.'

'Julius, is that really necessary?' asked Claude. 'Your mother will only be a moment.'

Whatever I say, whatever I do. But you can't very well stop me. Julius clambered out after his mother into cool air, the music and cheers sounding newly loud. *That's better.* In the distance he glimpsed sunlight flashing on brass instruments. *There's the band.* As the pavement was blocked with cheering women and children, he and Lilian began walking slowly behind the marchers – *Mother looks desperate* – when he heard a child's voice shout, 'Engländer, Engländer!' and, glancing round, Julius saw a small boy jumping up and pointing at him. *How does he know?* He looked back. *Of course, he's seen the GB plate on the car. Perhaps foreigners aren't supposed to be walking with the procession?* Then, though, a man just ahead of him turned, broke into a grin and reached out to shake Julius' hand. 'Heil Hitler,' called out another, with a tall feather sprouting from his hat. *I can't very well not.* Julius heiled back, raising his arm, and the man roared with delight. Now several hands reached back to shake his. *This is strange. And rather good, actually.*

By now they had drawn level with the bar and, seeing a gap between the cheering bystanders, Lilian hurried through. Julius took a step after her only to stop and turn back. *No, I think I'll keep going. I rather like all this.* As if in reward, he found himself being ushered into the rear of the parade. The man with the feather called out to others, Julius heard the word 'Engländer', he found himself met with smiles, handshakes and back-slaps, and then felt something being pressed into his hand. *A banner. And why not? In for a penny . . .* He saw a young woman smiling at him from the side of the road. *She looks a little like Linda. The same eyes.* Suddenly, for no reason he could understand, he was surprised by an urge to cry. *This crowd, these people, they're so . . .* He couldn't think of the words. *So kind and welcoming. I haven't felt like this for . . .* For how long? Forever? *It's the oddest thing. I've never been to this country in my life, I don't know it at all, I don't speak a word of the language, yet I feel as if these are my people. These Nazis can't be so bad. Just because Claude and Frank like them, that doesn't mean anything. And the Jew business will just be politics, which everyone knows is a lot of lies and nonsense. Will this Hitler fellow do anything bad to anyone?* Julius blinked. *No.* He broke into a smile. *Just as I thought.* For some reason he found himself thinking of his sister Harriet. *What would she say if she saw me walking along carrying a swastika?* He felt an urge to laugh. *But she shouldn't mind. These people don't seem rich – they look like workers. And didn't Claude say that Nazis are quite different from fascists? Just because I think Hitler's all right now doesn't mean I have to like Claude's awful BUF. Just think, Harriet, Hitler would probably loathe Lou's fiancé.*

A car horn beeped behind him and, turning, Julius saw that his mother was climbing back into the Austin, which was turning into a side road. Claude was gesturing furiously through the windscreen for him to come back. *To hell with you. I'm staying here with my new friends.* A thought came to him. *Of course – this must be the good thing the Predictor said would happen. Yes!* The radio-like voice, which was coming through a public address system, spoke again and was answered with more cheers from the crowd. Joining in, Julius felt more slaps on his back. *I wonder what I just cheered?* He felt like laughing. *A pity I left the Brownie in the car as I'd love to take a shot or two.*

The parade passed into a square – *what a pretty spot, and that's a lovely old tree* – where a figure in a pale-brown uniform was standing on a small podium. Still holding his banner, Julius found himself ushered to the front, where the man with the feather called out excitedly – Julius again caught the word 'Engländer' – causing the man on the podium to reach down and shake him energetically by the hand. Now the whole crowd was cheering. *I'd better do another heil. Gosh, they really loved that.*

After the man on the podium had delivered a short speech, to further cheering, the one with the feather pointed to a beer hall behind them. 'Bier, bier.'

Even I understand that. But this is awkward. Julius opened his wallet and pulled out a ten-shilling note. 'No German money.'

'Not necessary,' said a thin, balding man. 'The beer is from us.'

'Well, thank you.' A question came to Julius as if from nowhere. *Will I ever be sent back to the Mid-Wales?* He hesitated, wondering if he dared ask. *Courage.* He blinked both eyes. *No, you never will.* A deep joy and relief spread through him. *It said no, it said no! I'm never going back there.*

They had almost reached the beer hall when Julius saw someone pushing his way through the crowd. *Oh hell, trust you to turn up and spoil everything.*

'For goodness' sake,' demanded Claude, 'don't you know we're late for the winery?'

'But they want me to go and have a beer,' said Julius.

'Out of the question,' snapped his stepfather, but then the thin, balding man raised his nose high in the air and, mimicking Claude's intonation perfectly, repeated, 'Out of the question.' Loud laughter broke out all around.

Claude's livid. 'Sorry,' said Julius to those around him, handing over his banner, 'but I think I'd better go,' and he began following his stepfather, as arms reached out to shake his hand and slap his back.

'I don't know what you thought you were doing,' growled Claude as they walked.

Julius felt strangely exultant, almost fearless. 'Oh, stop being such an old misery.' *Look at his face. How you'd love to see me locked away. But you can't. The Predictor said so – it promised.*

'You looked like you were enjoying yourself,' said Lilian disapprovingly as he climbed back into the car.

I don't want to talk about it – not to you, Mother, not to any of you. It was my thing. But then Julius found words pouring out of him. 'It was wonderful. They were all so nice and kind. I really love this country, everything about it.'

'I thought you didn't like Nazis,' sneered Frank.

'That was before.' *You're just envious. You can't stand the thought that they all liked me so much.*

Claude did better with his map-reading and they soon reached the vineyard. In the tasting room, as Claude inspected, sniffed and spat, and Lilian, who spoke some German, helped translate the winemaker's explanations, Julius studied a picture on the wall of a uniformed figure staring into the distance, the name HITLER in large letters underneath. *There he is with his little moustache. He's not quite as I expected. He doesn't look dynamic like Claude said. If anything he looks blank, and perhaps a touch annoyed. If he was cast in a film, what would he play?* Julius peered at the photograph, mentally replacing his uniform with civilian clothes, only to see another uniform. *A ticket inspector on the railways. Yes, that's what he'd be. Harmless enough, I'd say.*

'A little on the sweet side, as German whites often are,' declared Claude as they drove on. 'But not bad, not bad at all. Yes, I'll certainly order a few cases, as I can see some of my customers lapping it up. And I have to say, I much prefer doing business with Germans. They play a straight bat.'

Because they made a fuss of you and nobody bit their tongue at your ridiculous-sounding French.

After visiting two wineries, their next destination was Frankfurt, a slight detour from their route which Lilian had requested, as she had fond memories of visiting it as a child. They arrived in the late afternoon and, after checking into their hotel, they set out to explore the old town, walking through small squares with fountains, and street after street of half-timbered houses. 'It says there are more than a thousand of them here,' said Claude, looking up from his Baedeker. 'It's thought to be the finest medieval old town in all Europe.'

'It's just as I remembered,' said Lilian. 'Isn't it adorable?'

For once, Julius agreed with his mother. *It is beautiful.* He got out the Brownie and took a couple of pictures.

'I have to say, people look much healthier here than they do in England,' Claude observed approvingly. 'They're fit and strong, with none of the idle, round-shouldered types you see in British cities.'

Frank had found a shop selling hunters' knives. 'These ones in the window look really good. But it's closed – there's a sign.'

Lilian peered at the words. 'No, it's all right. It says no Jews allowed.'

'Oh,' said Frank, happily pushing open the door.

That'll be nothing. Just one silly shopkeeper.

For dinner, they went to a beer cellar that had been recommended by the hotel, with a low ceiling and air that was thick with smells of drink, cooking and tobacco smoke.

And heil Hitler to you. And you, and you. See, they all love me here, too. They sat down and ordered drinks – Claude persuaded Frank to try some German beer – and, as Lilian translated the menu, Julius noticed they were catching glances from a family at the neighbouring table: a couple with their lanky, grown-up son. *Will they talk to us?* He blinked. *They will.* Sure enough, when Lilian had given their orders to the waiter, the father leaned towards them. *Yes! It's definitely working again. Hurrah!*

'Sorry to bother you, but are you by any chance English?'

Only someone English would say that. You know we are – otherwise you wouldn't have asked.

When Claude gave a nod, the man broke into a smile. 'I just wondered if you follow the football? I'm a Coventry man myself.'

'And me,' volunteered the lanky son.

'And though we're only in the third division south, we've had a pretty decent season so far, with a good chance of promotion. Only I haven't been able to find out how we did against Northampton last weekend. I've looked for English papers everywhere but I can't find anything.'

'I see,' said Claude with too much smile.

Wrong accents.

'I'm afraid I'm not a great follower of football,' Claude told them. 'How about you, Frank?'

'Not really. Cricket and rugby are more my thing.'

Posher.

'Oh, right,' said the father, disappointed.

The conversation might have ended there, but Lilian gave them a bright smile. 'Have you been in Germany long?'

Mustn't be rude to poor provincial folk. Not that they can be that poor if they're on holiday over here.

'Almost two weeks,' the father answered. 'We're just on our way home now.'

'And you've had a lovely time?'

'Not bad,' answered the man's wife. 'Though the weather's been quite poor. When we went to the Alps we hardly saw a thing.'

How dismal you are. Can't you see it's wonderful here?

'And all those castles and churches, I mean, they're nice at first, but once you've seen a few . . .' She hesitated.

You're worried Claude and Lilian will think you're uncultured. Too late. They already do.

'And people can be quite rude,' she went on. 'One man shouted at poor Len just because he hadn't saluted his flag.'

'Though he was nice enough when I said I was English,' said her husband.

'But you've seen the old town here?' asked Lilian hopefully. 'We thought it was absolutely enchanting.'

'Not bad,' said the father breezily. 'Of course, we have our share of nice old buildings back in Coventry.'

'And they don't have my sauce,' said the son.

His mother saw the others' confusion. 'HP, he means. He loves it.'

'I can't eat potatoes without it,' said the son, glancing glumly towards his plate, on which a pile of them lay abandoned.

Moan, moan, moan.

'I'd have brought some bottles over with us, if I'd only known,' his mother went on. 'None of the restaurants have it and we've tried all the shops, but it's just mustard, mustard, mustard.'

'I don't like mustard at all,' the son said glumly.

'Well, I think it's wonderful here,' Julius cut in. *Everyone's looking at me. Too loud? Should I stop?* But instead, he began talking about the parade he had joined that afternoon. 'They were all so friendly and welcoming. It's hard to explain.' *Claude and Frank look annoyed. First they were cross because I didn't like their Nazis, and now they're cross because I do. They want to keep them all to themselves.*

A voice broke in from another table, where two bearded men were sitting, both of whom looked as if they'd had a few beers. 'Germany good?'

'Yes, Germany good,' said Julius with enthusiasm.

'Very good indeed,' said Claude, louder.

Up went the two men's glasses, they chanted, 'Prost!' and Julius' family joined them.

Even though I've only got water.

The bearded man gave Julius an anxious, tentative look. 'Hitler good?'

Why ever not? 'Yes, Hitler good.'

'An absolute first-rate chap,' insisted Claude.

The Coventry father's asking for the bill. And good riddance. Why are those two on that table giving me a nasty look? Don't you like your Hitler? Shame on you.

'Here's to Germany and England, friends forever,' said Claude grandly and he snapped his fingers to order more beer.

An hour later, his stomach filled with pot roast, potatoes and cabbage, Julius stepped out of the beer cellar. *I won. Claude was louder but they liked me best. I could tell.*

'A damn fine evening,' Claude declared. 'And this time the schnapps really was free. I tell you, this is the country for me.'

Look how he's walking. You're drunk. I've never seen you like this before. And you're not much better, Mother. Nor you, Frank. You're all a disgrace to fascism.

'This is how Britain will be once we've taken charge,' said Claude, his voice loud in the quiet street. 'As Tom says,

"Britain First", and that's how it'll be. Out with alien financiers, out with the old gang of bankers and politicians.'

'Hurrah,' said Frank.

'We'll build a new corporatist Britain, neither communist nor capitalist.'

'Hurrah.'

You're like a two-man rally.

'Private liberty, public duty.'

'Hurrah.'

'You're rather loud,' said Lilian, a little uneasily.

Claude, though he lowered his voice, was too excited to stop. 'Master the machine to meet the modern fact.'

'Hurrah.'

'All for the state and the state for all.'

'Hurrah.'

What's that doing? A dark-grey van was parked further down the road ahead of them, and Julius could just hear the engine running. He felt suddenly uneasy. 'Perhaps we should turn down this road?'

'Nonsense,' Claude declared. 'The hotel's straight ahead.' He gave Frank a slap on the back. 'A Britain where men are men and women are women, free to pursue the important career of motherhood.'

'Hurrah.'

'A Britain where . . .' But even Claude and Frank had

noticed now, as two uniformed men had emerged from a house beside the van, pushing a third man before them, who, Julius could see from the awkward way he moved, was handcuffed. *I knew we should have gone the other way. But it'll all be fine, I'm sure it will. Are they police? I saw a policeman earlier and he had a different hat. These ones look more military. But they must be a kind of policeman. And who's she?* A woman had darted out of the building and was tugging at the coat of the rearmost man in uniform. *No, don't do that. Go back, please.* Julius tried to look away but he couldn't help but watch. The man whose coat she had grabbed turned, raised his hand and gave her a quick, brutal slap, so she fell back and was left sitting on her haunches on the pavement, looking almost comical. *There'll be a good reason. Of course there will.*

The prisoner, crying out at what he had just seen, tried to break free and reach her but failed and he was bundled into the back of the van like a sack. The two in uniform climbed in after him, slamming shut the doors. For a moment all was quiet, aside from the faint moans of the woman, still kneeling on the ground, but then, as Julius and his family came nearer, the van began moving, rocking slightly on its wheels in an odd, jerking movement, as if it were engaged in some form of strange callisthenics. Julius could just hear, with each movement, a faint, flat sound, like a leather ball being bounced.

Julius struggled. *It'll be something else. They're arranging things in the van. That'll be it.*

'Let's cross the road,' said Claude, a grim look on his face, and they did so, keeping as far as they could from the woman whimpering on her knees and the gently rocking van. Even Frank looked shaken. 'Not pretty, I dare say,' said Claude, as they walked on. 'But then we don't know who they were.'

'Reds, probably,' said Frank a little breathlessly. 'Or spies.'

Something terrible. They must be. Criminals. Rapists. Robbers or kidnappers. Gangsters. Murderers.

'Subversives, certainly,' agreed Claude. 'A danger to the state, no question. And that sort of thing has to be dealt with. Though I have to say that when it's our turn, we'll do it a lot more cleanly than that.'

'Is the hotel far?' asked Lilian, her voice shrill. 'It's been a long day and I'm awfully tired.'

They didn't look like subversives or spies. They looked quite like you two. But then, just in time, another thought came to Julius' rescue. *But that doesn't mean anything. They must've been in disguise.*

*

They left Frankfurt early the next morning, as Sam needed to reach Munich in time to catch his train back to London. As they drove, all in the car were silent. *They're probably hung-over. They should have kept to water like me. Or they're thinking about that dark grey . . .* With an effort, Julius pushed the thought away. *Isn't it beautiful here? The hills. The trees just breaking into spring leaves. A bit later here than back home.* Julius' eyes lit upon a man riding on an old bicycle. *Predictor, what will happen to him?* He blinked. *He'll become a chef and have his own restaurant in Berlin.* Smiling now, Julius saw a young woman walking a small dog. *And her?* Another blink. *She'll be a doctor and will discover a cure for a terrible disease.* They passed through a small town where, in the window of a shop, Julius glimpsed a girl and a young man rearranging a display of musical instruments. *And them, Predictor?* He blinked. *They'll get married. Next spring. And they'll have three children. Two boys and a girl. The oldest will be called Hans.* Julius felt an urge to laugh. 'Yes, Hans.'

'What's going on back there?' asked Claude.

Oops, I said it out loud. How did I do that?

'He's talking to himself,' said Frank. 'He just said hands.'

Claude twisted round in his seat, looked like he was about to say something but then settled for a warning glare.

As if I care. I'm safe now. The Predictor said so.

In Munich they said their farewells to Sam and checked

into the hotel, where Claude announced, importantly, that he had to slip off for a little while. 'One of my hush-hush jaunts.'

'D'you want me to come along too?' offered Frank.

You're trying not to seem desperate to go.

'I think better not this time,' said Claude.

Quite right, Stepfather, you can't go visiting the Nazis with your spotty schoolboy son. Frank's biting his lip and looks like he's close to tears. No blubbering now, Little Frank. Come on, man, buck up! A thought came to Julius. *Claude should really take me along. I'm sure Hitler would love me, like everybody here does.*

Lilian had seen her son's distress. 'We can go and find a lovely café,' she said soothingly, 'and have some tea and some cakes. They do such good ones here. You can have some cocoa – you love cocoa.'

Mother, how could you? You've made him feel like a little boy just when he wanted to be the big man, going off with his father to meet the famous Hitler. Poor Frank – I almost feel sorry for you. But come to think of it, I'd quite like to try some Munich cakes.

Yet there was no time for cakes, as it turned out. Claude left them, and Julius was still unpacking his suitcase when outside in the corridor, he heard footsteps that he recognized: a thumping sort of step that always seemed a little surprising in one whose face had such an aura of delicate, romantic dreaminess. *Maude.*

Everyone assembled in Lilian and Claude's room for greetings. *Even I get a hug. Maude doesn't seem disgusted like Frank does, but more sorry for me. That's something, I suppose. Where have I seen that look before?* Julius remembered a family catastrophe many years back when the Labrador had been hit by a car. *The vet had to put him down. I hope that's not what you'd like for me, Maude.* Remembering her dream of being called to Hitler's table at the tea rooms, Julius began telling her of his adventure with the parade in the small town, only to feel disappointed. *I thought she'd be excited but she's hardly even listening.*

She turned to Frank. 'Did you bring the Slimers?'

Frank triumphantly pulled a decrepit box from his pocket.

Oh no. I thought they'd fallen apart years ago.

The Slimers were a set of playing cards that Frank, Maude and Harriet had had since they were small. Over time, each card had become so stained and bent that they were valued not for playing conventional games, but for permitting feats of memory, as all three players could identify most cards from their pattern side. Many had acquired their own names, inspired by their deformities and past misadventures. 'Shall we have a quick game?' said Maude.

'Why not?' agreed Frank.

But once again, events thwarted plans. They had barely dealt out a hand when Claude returned, greeting Maude with a kiss.

You don't look happy at all.

'A damnable secretary. Who told me that, most unfortunately, everybody was awfully busy today, though I could always come back and try again tomorrow if I want. I do not want. Demeaning myself like that.'

I knew he should have brought me along.

'I mean, I wasn't expecting to see Hitler himself . . .'

You were.

'. . . but I did think I'd at least get to meet someone of rank. Not for myself, of course, as I don't give a fig . . .'

You do.

'. . . but to shw proper respect to Tom.'

So Hitler doesn't like your BUF. Another thing that tells me he can't be such a bad sort.

'I know who's responsible for this insult,' said Claude bitterly. 'It's those sneaking-about-in-the-shadows types back home, who go spreading lies about poor Cimmie.'

Cimmie?

Julius didn't need to ask, as Maude didn't know either.

'Tom's wife,' Claude explained. She had died just a year earlier, of peritonitis, Claude recounted, but Mosley's enemies had shown no respect for her, even in death, and repeated lies that her ancestors were Jewish, though her grandfather, whose name was Levi, was in fact from a family of Swiss Mennonites. 'Those coves often have queer names. But nobody cares a fig for the truth these days, more's the pity,' said Claude. 'Throw some dirt and it'll stick, and never mind that it's the basest invention.'

'Poor Pa,' said Maude in her flat, monotone voice, but then she broke into a smile. 'I know what. I'll give Karl a ring.' Seeing the others' curious looks, she explained how she had been introduced to Karl the previous summer at a London drinks party. 'He and his wife are so sweet. They've had me to lunch three times. He's not one of the high-ups but he knows them all. He was one of the very first to join the party, back when it was just starting. He showed me his card once and his number was just ninety something, which anyone would kill for these days. And he's introduced me to no end of absolutely fascinating people. I'm sure he'll be able to help.'

'Why not? Let's give him a try, Maudie,' said Claude, with a half-smile.

You're pleased but you're also annoyed that your twenty-year-old daughter is better connected than you are.

Claude and Maude went down to reception to use the telephone, but on their return their expressions were quite unchanged – Maude excited and Claude sour. 'Karl said all the bigwigs are awfully busy with something just now,' she explained to the others. 'But then he was terribly nice. He said there's a tour going to Dachau tomorrow and he thinks he can get us places.'

'Dachau?' asked Lilian. 'Is that where they do the operas?'

'No,' said Maude, laughing. 'That's Bayreuth.' Dachau, she explained, was one of the new camps that had been set up across the country, where undesirables were sent to be remade as good, patriotic citizens. 'You know, Reds, queers, Gypsies, cheating Jews, that sort of thing,' said Maude. 'I think at Dachau they're mostly Reds. The Nazis are terribly proud of the place and they love showing it off.'

Undesirables? Julius felt a twinge of panic. *No, everyone loves me here. And it sounds a good thing. Turning these poor chaps around. I'd like to see it.*

'I'm not sure I can,' grumbled Claude.

Maude gave him a stern look. 'Don't be such a sourpuss, Pa. Karl's being very kind. And I'm sure it'll be awfully interesting. You should see what they're doing here.'

Claude shrugged. 'I suppose.'

Lilian was worried about Maude missing her classes at the Baroness's school.

You'd rather go and see something pretty.

But Maude insisted the Baroness wouldn't mind in the slightest. 'We're always going off on trips to learn about

Germany and German culture. She'll be hugely impressed. And none of the other girls at the school has been. They'll all be frightfully jealous.'

Yes! Will it be a good thing, Predictor? Stooping down, pretending to retie his shoelace, Julius blinked. *Yes. It'll be a very good thing and you'll have a splendid day.*

The next morning, just on time, a bus appeared in front of the hotel. Julius, the Brownie on his lap, sat in the row behind Frank and Maude as they drove through the city, collecting more passengers. At the third hotel a girl took the seat beside him and introduced herself as Sophie.

Nice face.

'So what's brought you here?' she asked.

'My family. They're all in the BUF. You know, Mosley's outfit.'

She gave him a wary glance. 'And you?'

'No, not me.'

'Why not?'

Julius found it hard to think. 'I don't think they'd take me.'

She looked at him for a moment and then broke into peals of laughter. 'You're the funniest fellow.'

I don't really know why. But does it matter? How nice it

feels to be sitting on a bus next to a girl. See, the Predictor was right. He tried to think when he'd last done such a thing. *Two years ago? When I took Linda home from the studio? Just before . . . ?* He mentally changed the subject. *That was one of the worst things about the Mid-Wales. We knew there were women in the other wing but we never saw them. Except sometimes when I was going to the farm and I'd catch sight of them in the distance. Or when Orderly Davies took us to the pub in Talgarth. He'd always say before we set out, 'I know it's not often you see a pair of titties, boys, but try not to gawp, eh?'*

Sophie gave him a confiding look. 'It's the same with me.' She gestured towards a greying, tweedy couple sitting stiffly in their seats across the aisle. 'Father's mad keen on Hitler and always refers to him as "Our Adolf". Then I'm sure only true believers get a seat on this bus. Reds and leftie journalists won't get anywhere near.'

'You're going to trump me with Squashed Wasp,' Julius heard Frank say from the row ahead.

'But then you'll play Blackberry Jam,' said Maude. 'No, it's worse, you'll play Gutter Water.'

Should I tell Sophie about the procession? I don't want to feel I'm fibbing to her. But this is so nice and I don't want to spoil it.

Then the chance had passed as she asked him about his

work. 'How wonderful. I love the pictures.' She asked what films he had worked on, and which actors and directors he had met. 'Edna Berger? I just adore her.'

The bus came to a stop. *Are we already there? I thought it would be much further. That's a shame.*

Everyone was getting up and Sophie did the same, giving him a little wave. 'See you later.'

I wonder if I'll sit next to her on the way back. He blinked. *You will, Julius, you will.*

The tourists assembled in front of the closed wooden gates of the entrance. *The huge eagle and swastika above are a bit fake-looking – they could be on a film set – but they're very striking in their way. And this chap must be our guide. Smart black outfit.* 'Heil Hitler,' Julius replied. *Sophie didn't do one and now she's giving me a look. But I'm sure she'll change her mind when she sees how nice everyone is.*

The guide, who introduced himself as Captain Hauptmann, went through a typed list, checking the tourists' names, and saluting anyone with a military rank. Julius' stepfather he greeted respectfully as 'Major Reid of the British Union of Fascists'.

Claude loves that, of course.

The guide began explaining, in excellent English, that the camp was the first of its kind and had been opened a year ago, shortly after Hitler became chancellor, that it was where guards were trained before being sent to other camps across the Reich and that, like all such camps, it was temporary and would be closed when the Bolshevik threat had been overcome. *I hope this isn't going to be boring. I'm sure it won't be.* Julius felt his mind drifting. *When was I last on something like this? The school tour of Welsh castles. Mr Parker would make us wait in front of the moat, just like Captain Hauptmann here, and tell us who'd built the castle and when, before he finally let us run in and clamber over everything. Mr Parker could go on a bit, too. Though of course he wasn't at all like Captain Hauptmann – a little round man.*

'Very good way of putting it,' murmured Claude. 'I should tell Tom.'

What did I miss? Julius could still hear the guide's last words in his head, like a gramophone recording: '. . . how much better than communists, who don't bother to reform anyone but just shoot them.' *See – kindly, just like I thought.* He glanced at Sophie, but she was looking away.

The guide had seen Julius' Brownie. 'I must ask you, no photographs, please.'

'Oh, of course.' *There probably won't be anything to take anyway.* The wooden gates were swung open, the group walked inside and something caught Julius' eye. *Watchtowers? I suppose they have to have those. Nothing so wrong with that.*

The tour rounded a corner to face a parade ground with a crowd of men standing in rows. Julius felt himself gasp. *Their clothes – it's just like the Mid-Wales. Old suits that don't fit. Though some seem like they're in old police uniforms. They're all very thin, but then we were pretty thin, too, I suppose. I'm surprised they don't turn their heads and look. At the Mid-Wales we were always curious to see outsiders.* A guard shouted commands, the prisoners snapped to attention in unison and then began a series of drill movements. *So it's like the army. Of course – that'll be why they didn't turn their heads.*

Sophie had appeared beside him. 'They must've been waiting out here for us for ages. And we were late, too.'

A Dutch couple had got the time wrong and had had to be extricated from their breakfast.

'They might not have been.' *She's frowning.*

At a final shouted order, the parade dispersed and the guide took the group into one of the many accommodation huts. *Just one washbasin for the whole hut? There must be a lot of queuing. The bedding doesn't look up to much, and they don't have big windows like we did. And it smells worse even than our ward. But it's not all that bad. And at least they won't get jungle juice each evening.*

'I think I might go outside for a moment,' said Lilian with a strained smile. 'It's rather close in here.'

You wouldn't have liked the smell of our ward, either, Mother.

'Reeking Reds,' said Frank, making Claude laugh.

The guide had heard and misunderstood. 'You may think the conditions here are tough, but there's no point in dealing softly with an enemy that has no scruples, and who would think nothing of murdering every one of you. No, I'd say we're very gentle here. We give these people a second chance, which is more than Bolsheviks ever do.'

See, they're gentle, Sophie. She's still frowning.

They set out towards a factory-like building that dwarfed the rest, where they were to see workshops. *She'll like this better, I'm sure. I always liked our farm. Mostly, anyway.* The group passed into a room where prisoners were repairing shoes, and then into another where they were making wooden beer mugs.

'You're welcome to buy these at the end of the tour,' the guide explained. 'And I promise that they're excellent value, not expensive at all.' A few people laughed and Julius felt an urge to join in but then, thinking of Sophie, he stopped himself. Leading the group to one of the work desks, the guide turned to the tourists. 'Do we have a German-speaker here? I should explain. We have so many lies written about our camp by all the Jewish newspapers that I want you to see this is the real truth.'

Maude? Mother won't.

Sure enough, Maude's face broke into a sleepy smile and up went her hand, but a young man with a double chin at the front of the group was quicker. The guide addressed a prisoner at the end of the table, who hurriedly got to his feet to reply. 'He says,' translated the volunteer, 'that life here isn't bad so long as you follow the rules.'

See. It's not too awful at all.

'This is all wrong,' Sophie murmured. 'Don't you see? The one he's questioning isn't half as thin and haggard as the rest and seems very well fed. And the inmates look at one another but they won't look at him. I don't think he's a real prisoner at all.'

That can't be right. 'Really?'

'Ask him what he'll do when he's released,' said the guide.

Back came the translated answer. 'He says he'll get a job and then he'll join the National Socialist Party.'

'Good man,' said Claude.

Predictor, is Sophie right about that man? Julius blinked. *No. Oh good. I thought not.*

'As you see,' said the guide, 'our efforts here are not without result.'

'This place gives me the willies,' said Sophie.

'I'm sure we'll be finished soon.'

But next there was lunch. 'Don't expect too much,' the

guide told them as they walked on. 'We have simple food here – simple food to make healthy minds.' His face broke into a conspiratorial smile. 'But for our guests there may also be a little simple wine.'

Claude pulled a face and Lilian laughed. 'Don't be such an awful snob.'

'I'm surprised they take so much trouble over a lot of Reds,' said Frank and Maude widened her eyes in agreement.

But Claude was more forgiving. 'I'd say it's worth it, if some of them can be brought back into the fold. Like that prisoner chap just now.'

'Are they yours?' asked Sophie.

How did she guess? I suppose I look like them. 'Yes.'

'Poor you.'

The guide said the camp would be closed when the communist threat is gone. When will that be? Julius blinked and back came the answer. *In a year's time, on the seventeenth of April 1935. That's not too far away.*

'It was nice watching them making the beer mugs,' said Lilian.

'Yes, that was very good to see,' agreed Claude. 'Old-fashioned craftsmanship. A change from those awful American factory lines.' He paused, smiling. 'I might get us one, Pet, as a souvenir.'

'Lovely.'

Mother doesn't want a souvenir. Not after the accommodation hut.

In the mess hall they were led to a long table on a raised platform, where they were greeted by the camp's officers, as prisoners shuffled to their tables below. Claude was ushered to sit next to the commandant.

Next to the chief. You love that.

'It's just like high table at my old college at Cambridge,' Claude declared with a laugh.

As Julius had hoped, he found himself sitting next to Sophie. *Where does this place remind me of? The dining room in the Mid-Wales? Not really, as this is many times larger.* Then he remembered. *The banquet scene in Waltzing in Warsaw. It had filled the whole studio and the tables had been set out much as they were here. It was easily the costliest scene in the picture. I was so worried something would go wrong. And then the director wanted the bride and groom to walk in with all the other guests following, which made no sense and would have looked terrible. I had to fight like hell to talk him out of it. I wonder how it all turned out?*

'Look at the prisoners' food,' murmured Sophie. 'It's quite different from what we're getting.'

It looks like soup, though it's hard to tell from here. Does it have to be the same?

'Lots of writers,' Claude said to the camp commandant. 'H. G. Wells. The chap who wrote Tarka the Otter.'

'Viele Schriftsteller,' Captain Hauptmann translated.

'And didn't you say Shaw, too?' added Lilian.

Claude laughed. 'No, he's a leftie, though he's not at all keen on the Jews.' He pondered. 'Newspaper chaps. Beaverbrook and Rothermere.'

'Zeitungsverleger. Beaverbrook und Rothermere.'

Of course – it's everyone who likes the BUF.

'And Prince Edward, our future king.'

'Und Prinz Edward, unser zukünftiger König.'

The commandant gave a respectful nod.

Sophie's father asked the guide if corporal punishment was used in the camp.

'Only when necessary, to enforce discipline.'

'My pa looks quite disappointed,' said Sophie. 'He'd like to think of the Reds getting a good thrashing.'

After pudding appeared, they were given schnapps and finally it was time to leave.

'Thank God,' murmured Sophie as they filed out of the building.

It wasn't so bad.

They were already halfway back to the gate when Julius remembered. *Damn.* 'I'm awfully sorry,' he said to the guide. 'But I must've left my camera in the dining room. It's all right, I know my way back.' *He looks annoyed. And Claude's rolling his eyes.*

'Lieutenant Hoffmann here will go with you,' Captain Hauptmann told him.

That doesn't sound like an offer, more an order. As you like. Julius began walking back with the guard at his side. *Am I supposed to salute? All the prisoners are saluting us. But Lieutenant Hoffmann isn't. It's funny – it feels different now that it's just me. In a group you're in your own little world. The prisoners seem awfully nervous of us, darting out of our way. Don't worry, I'm not going to hurt you. I suppose this Hoffman's quite a big chap.* A prisoner who had been kneeling, tying his shoelace, glanced up, caught sight of them, jumped to his feet looking panicked, saluted and flitted out of their path. *I suppose it's all that army stuff. Stand up straight, polish your boots, that sort of thing. Not that their shoes are shiny here.*

Walking into the mess hall, Julius found a group of prisoners was at work clearing the lunch table of plates and, seeing Julius and the lieutenant, they jumped stiffly to attention. *There's my chair and, oh good, there's the Brownie underneath, just where I left it.* A prisoner was crouched on the ground, his back to them, furiously scrubbing at a patch on the floor. 'Excuse me,' said Julius, stooping down to reach for the Brownie. Turning round, the man stared at him with wide eyes and hurriedly began crawling backwards, knocking into a table leg. In that instant Julius felt a sudden sense of recognition. *That look.* He had seen it so many times in the Mid-Wales on the faces of patients. *The ones who had terrors. What are you so frightened of? Not me, surely?* Julius straightened up, turned, and glancing round he saw the same look was on the face of every prisoner. For a moment he struggled – *they're probably just . . .* but then the thought faded, abandoning him. *Oh God, oh God. How come I didn't see before?* One of the prisoners turned to move a chair from his path and, through tears in his shirt, Julius glimpsed his back. *Is that a tattoo? It's like a big purple spider. No, it's not a tattoo. Oh God.*

'Alles gut?' asked Lieutenant Hoffmann.

'Yes, absolutely.' *Sophie knew.* He thought of the gently rocking van. *How did I ever think . . . ?* The parade came to him and for an instant he felt a kind of longing but then it slipped away. *How could I? I need to talk to Sophie.*

He walked out of the mess hall and found himself troubled anew. *But I don't understand. The Predictor said everything would be all right and that this would be a good day. Was it lying? Unless it wasn't the Predictor at all and I was asking something else? Some other thing that means me harm.* A strange movement ahead caught Julius' eye. *What's wrong with him?* A hunched prisoner with stringy black hair, wearing a ragged brown suit, was coming towards him, staggering a little as he walked. Saluting, he veered one way and then another.

'Hey,' shouted Lieutenant Hoffmann, and Julius stepped out from the man's path only for him to swerve sharply at the last moment, colliding with Julius.

'Es tut mir leid, es tut mir leid!' the prisoner begged, saluting again as he limped away.

'Halt,' roared Lieutenant Hoffmann. 'Karte.'

Oh God. 'But I'm fine,' Julius insisted, trying to smile. *His eyes – that same look. He's shaking.* 'Really, I'm absolutely all right. It was nothing.' *Don't hurt him, I beg you.*

Led by the lieutenant's wagging finger, the prisoner stepped forwards holding out a piece of grubby cardboard.

He'll hit him. 'It was nothing, really, nothing at all.' *No, he's just looking at the man's card, thank God. But what if he seeks him out later, when nobody's here to see? I bet he will. It's there on his face.*

Julius felt a shudder of relief as he finally walked back beneath the eagle and swastika and out of the camp gate. *They're already on the bus. Don't go without me!* He hurried towards it, hardly responding to Lieutenant Hoffmann's goodbye, and saw that another camp guard was clambering aboard ahead of him, one hand supporting a tray stacked with wooden beer mugs. As Julius got on, the guard began handing these out, putting on a little show as he did so, holding them with great care, as if he were a waiter in a beer hall and each was filled to the brim with foaming beer. *How can they laugh?*

'You have your camera, I see,' said the guide.

'Yes, thank you, everything's fine.'

'That's good.'

Claude, taking his mug, pulled out his wallet. 'How much do I owe you, Captain?'

'No charge, Major. It's our little gift.'

'Well, that's jolly nice of you.'

Someone's sitting next to Sophie. It was the German translator with the double chin. Julius caught a few of his words as he went by.

'. . . though Mercedes have sold best for us lately . . .'

Sophie gave Julius a quick roll of her eyes.

Another thing that it promised. Everything's gone wrong. He took the last empty seat, next to a large man with a broad smile who introduced himself as a minister from the American Midwest. As the bus set off he told Julius all about his hometown. 'It's a great little place. You'd love it, Julius, I just know you would.'

It sounds just like you – wholesome, devout, confident. Why haven't you said anything about this camp? Or did you think it was all perfectly fine? A troubling thought came to Julius. *Then I might have too, if I hadn't left the camera behind.*

The bus stopped at Sophie's hotel and Julius watched as she and her parents got up from their seats and she gave him a wave goodbye. Shortly afterwards it was his family's turn.

'I don't have to go back to the Baroness today,' said Maude as they made their way out to the street, 'and it's still only half past two. I could give you a little tour of Munich if you like. It's a lovely place.'

'That sounds a jolly good idea,' agreed Claude.

'Awfully nice,' agreed Lilian, her voice still shrill, 'a dear old church or two,' and Maude began leading the way.

Should I tell them? Julius blinked. *Maybe. Maybe? What sort of answer is that? How dare it desert me when I really need it?* And then, without having meant to, he found he was blurting out words, recounting what he had seen.

'But of course they'll be scared,' said Claude. 'That's the whole idea. Otherwise they'd never change their ways.'

'But the man with the back?' said Julius.

'What about it?' said Frank. 'The guide told us they do that sort of thing.'

Your glistening eyes. You like the thought of someone having his back torn to pieces.

'He was probably one of those zealots,' said Claude. 'The kind who simply won't listen to reason.'

Julius felt a rare kinship with his mother. *I could do with seeing something pretty, too.* But both of them had misjudged Maude's notion of a city tour. After a few minutes' walking they stopped in front of a bulky, old-fashioned-looking building with a large swastika flag flying from the roof, another draped down above the main door, and more to each side. It was beginning to rain.

'This is a place I really don't need to see again,' said Claude sourly.

'Pa, I'm so sorry. I should have thought,' said Maude. Seeing the others' wondering looks, she told them it was the Brown House, the Nazi party headquarters. The rain was growing heavier, making a slight hissing noise on the pavement.

'Perhaps we should ask if we can go in?' wondered Lilian.

'I'm damned if I will,' said Claude.

Julius felt something rustle in his jacket pocket. *It feels like paper. How odd.* Pulling it out he found a thin wad of pages, each covered with lines of small, spidery handwriting. *How did that get there?* A raindrop landed on it, dissolving the ink of a word, and he put it back.

The rain was beginning to roar. 'There's a shop over there,' said Maude, breaking into a run. 'We'll smell like wet dogs,' she laughed as they stepped inside. It was a bookshop and was empty aside from the greying, bespectacled salesman.

'Können wir hier bleiben bis der Regen aufhört?' asked Maude.

'Of course,' the bookseller answered in English, making her smile. 'Stay as long as you like. Though I have one condition. I hope you will permit me to practise my English.'

'Certainly.'

Julius glanced at the pages he had found in his pocket. *It's German. I must have picked it up by accident. Though I can't think how. At the hotel?*

Claude was by the window, peering out at the street. 'It already looks like it might be stopping.'

I should ask Maude what it is.

But she was talking to the bookseller. 'So let me guess,' he asked. 'You are from London?'

Julius slipped the pages back into his pocket.

'Sort of,' said Maude. 'The edge. Kingston.'

'But I know it,' said the bookseller proudly. 'I was there once before the war. It was very lovely by the river.'

'We like it,' agreed Lilian.

'Happier days.' The bookseller's face grew thoughtful. 'With English people I always feel I can speak freely. It's not so easy in these times.'

Julius could see where the man's words were going. *But you don't know what kind of English these are.* 'You have a beautiful shop here,' he broke in.

'Thank you. But I'm afraid I don't have all the beautiful books I would like.'

'What d'you mean?' asked Maude coolly.

He still hasn't seen.

'Because many good books are no longer permitted here.'

Maude fixed him with a hard stare.

'I have to say, much though I love my country . . .'

'My family are all great admirers of Hitler's new Germany,' Julius interrupted. *The look on his face. I could be back in the camp.*

'As am I, of course,' said the bookseller quickly.

A cry rang out from the other side of the shop. 'I don't believe it. Him!' Claude was staring furiously out of the window.

Will Maude report him? Julius blinked. *Maybe. Maybe, maybe? Not again!*

'You see the fellow who's walking out of the Brown House with those three Nazi chaps,' Claude told the others, as they went over to join him. 'He's one of Arnold Leese's crowd.' Julius saw a thin, hunched man in a raincoat raising his arm to salute three stiffly uniformed figures. 'It's an absolute disgrace,' said Claude. 'They refuse to see me, though I represent the largest and most dynamic fascist party in Britain, but they're happy to have a chinwag with that useless nobody.' Arnold Leese, Claude explained, ran a rival group to the BUF, the Imperial Fascist League. 'A nonsense little outfit if ever there was one. In fact not long ago we sent over some of the biff boys to knock their HQ about and give them a good hiding. But Leese really hates the Jews. He's a vet, and the world expert on some kind of camel and he gets very hot under the collar about kosher slaughtering. And of course he doesn't have Mussolini breathing down his neck. He'll be the one peddling lies about poor Cimmie.' Claude shook his head. 'I can't believe the Nazis are talking to his lot and not me. It's outrageous.'

Poor Claude. Outdone by some fascists even nastier than yours.

Maude went over and leaned against his shoulder, 'Poor Pa,' and Frank and Lilian stood nearer too.

They've framed themselves around him like a painting. The perfect family.

'At least it's stopped raining,' said Lilian.

Maude shot the bookseller a hard stare as they left. Then, as they stepped into the street, her face grew suddenly animated. 'I know what you should do, Pa,' she said, 'to shut up this dreadful camel man. Forget about the Brown

House. You should go straight to the top and talk to Hitler.'

Claude frowned. 'And how will I do that?'

'We'll go to the Carlton Tea Rooms, of course,' she said brightly. 'Hitler goes there all the time. He even has his own table. Hans said he's in Munich just now so there's a very good chance he'll be there.'

Hitler himself – oh God.

Maude thought for a moment, calculating. 'It's Thursday today. I've seen him there at least eight times on Thursdays.'

The others were all looking at her.

'I go whenever I can,' she told them simply. 'My friend Dot and I have two shillings on which of us he'll call over to his table first.' Her face fell a little. 'Though he's always so busy chatting with his chums that he never casts a glance towards either of us.'

Poor Maude.

Already she had brightened again. 'He has the most extraordinary eyes. People say he can look into your face just for a second and he knows everything about you. Absolutely everything. I can believe it, too.'

Unasked, cakes came into Julius' thoughts, remembered from her letter. *The apple strudel is your favourite and then the chocolate. You don't like the sponge cake at all as it's too dry.*

Claude was cautiously interested. 'I have some BUF cards

in my wallet. I suppose I could have the waiter take one over to him.'

'Exactly,' said Maude excitedly. 'And I could go over with you.'

'Perhaps,' agreed Claude.

No.

'This is an excellent idea,' said Claude, warming to the notion. 'Take the bull by the horns. That's Tom's way. Go over the heads of these useless pen-pushers and straight to the man who counts. Then Arnold Leese's shower of a fellow can be swept away for the dross he is.'

Maude put out an arm to stop them, and pointed to a portico just ahead, that contained a couple of statues of military figures in antique uniforms. 'This is the tomb of all the poor chaps who were killed in Hitler's putsch. Everyone has to salute, even foreigners.'

Julius saw that on one side of the portico there was a modern addition, with a swastika and eagle, and a plaque that was hung with wreaths. Two soldiers stood guard. *That's the last thing I feel like doing – another Heil Hitler.*

Maude strode ahead and showed the others how it should be done, taking several steps towards the monument, where she raised her arm in a stiff salute, called out, 'Heil Hitler' in a ringing voice, and then bowed her head for a moment, as if in prayer, before walking swiftly on. Frank did a brisk salute and Julius watched as a portly man on a bicycle tried to salute as he rode by, only to swerve and almost fall off. *Nobody's laughing. Nobody's looking at him. It's dangerous even to laugh at a fat man nearly falling off his bike.* The cyclist's swerving reminded Julius of someone – *the man with the stringy hair who knocked into me in the camp* – and all at once he realized. *He was the one who put these pages in my pocket. Of course. He bashed into me on purpose to do it – that's why he was swerving back and forth. But what can it be?* Julius pulled the pages an inch out of his pocket, glimpsing the spidery writing. *A letter? Or some kind of notes.* He felt a new hope. *It could be important. I bet it is. Just think of the risk he took getting it to me. Thank goodness I didn't show it to Maude.*

'What d'you think you're doing, man?' called out Claude.

With a start, Julius realized he was walking past the monument and the two guards were glaring at him. He quickly turned, raised his arm and shouted Heil Hitler. *Damn. I wanted to do a bad one.* As he walked on, he looked again at the top edge of the pages and a worrying thought came to him. *What if we're all called over to see Hitler? What if he looks into my face and knows about this letter, or whatever it is? Should I just chuck it in the gutter? But then somebody might see. And I can't let down Stringy Hair after the danger he put himself in.* Maude was opening the door of the tea rooms. *Too late now. Will Hitler have me arrested and thrown into that camp?* He blinked. *Maybe. Ugh!* Walking through the door, for an instant he felt a kind of resentment. *Why did Stringy Hair have to pick me, of all people?*

Maude, as a regular customer, was given a warm smile by the waitress. As she led them to their table Julius saw, across the room, an empty one with a large card that read RESERVIERT FÜR DEN FÜHRER. *Surely he wouldn't have me arrested, as that could be some kind of diplomatic incident? I should do something. Kill him? He's the one behind that camp, and who's putting those looks on everyone's faces.* Julius, with little sense of intention, glanced about him for weapons but all he could see were dainty-looking chairs and a sugar bowl.

'Oh no,' said Maude as they sat down. 'It's Bessie Lydham.' She nodded her head towards a laughing girl several tables away. 'The one with the black hair and the snub nose. She'll ruin everything.'

Claude looked alarmed. 'What d'you mean?'

'She's absolutely awful,' said Maude bitterly. 'She's at another school but I'm always running into her, more's the pity. I've seen her sitting right there, pulling faces at poor Herr Hitler. And she once drew moustaches and silly glasses all over a copy of Der Stürmer. She showed it to me, with no shame at all.'

Some kind of magazine?

'I'm surprised she gets away with that sort of thing,' said Claude ponderously.

'I don't think Hitler notices her,' said Maude sorrowfully. 'He's always so busy with his chaps.' Her expression hardened. 'She should be deported, really she should.'

But Bessie Lydham had no opportunity to pull faces that day, any more than Claude had a chance to forge a connection with the Nazis, or Julius had reason to fear the Führer's all-seeing gaze. Though he and his family stayed long enough to consume several pots of tea and a good number of cakes, Hitler's table remained empty. At five-thirty Maude gave a sad shake of her head. 'He's never come in as late as this.'

'A shame,' said Claude.

Thank heavens.

Claude was in the process of paying the bill when a tall, thin man with a beaky nose appeared. 'I hoped I might find you here,' he said, standing over their table.

'Karl, how lovely,' said Maude brightly.

Does he know about the document? Julius blinked. *Maybe. Ugh.*

'Maude tells me that you will all be leaving for Austria tomorrow?' said Karl.

Claude nodded.

And thank goodness.

'As it happens,' said Karl, 'I have a little favour that I'd like to ask of you.'

Will everything get better now? Julius blinked. *Maybe.*

'I mean, it's a bit rich,' said Claude when Karl had gone and they began walking back to the hotel. 'They won't see me, though they see Leese's chap, and now this Karl wants me to smuggle their propaganda into Austria. I've half a mind to say no.'

Lilian wasn't keen either. 'I'm really not sure it's a good idea. I mean, what if we're caught?'

Maude laughed. 'Ma, stop being such a wet rag. They're not going to bother anyone in a British car. And we absolutely must do it, as Karl has been so very sweet to me. Besides, isn't this exactly the sort of thing that will make them keener to be friends with the BUF?'

'I suppose so,' Claude grumbled.

Later, at the hotel, when Frank went off to have a bath, Julius carefully examined the mysterious document, which he found was comprised of six pages. *The writing's very odd.* Examining it more closely, he saw that every other line was written upside down, so each page could be used twice. *It must be very hard to find paper in the camp. He was probably carrying it around for ages, waiting for a moment when he could pass it to a visitor like me. And all the while he'll have been terrified that one of the guards would search him.* It wasn't addressed to anybody, so it clearly wasn't a letter, though it was signed with a name, Joachim Holt. *So that's who you are, man with the stringy hair.* On one page, surrounded by tiny handwriting, was a delicate drawing of a small bird perched on barbed wire. *That's not bad, not bad at all.* On the last page, in tiny letters beneath the signature, Julius was surprised to find a few words in English. 'Please dear visitor, send this to the Manchester Guardian.'

Julius felt a rush of hope. *The Manchester Guardian?* He frowned in concentration. *Is this document important?* He blinked. *Yes.* He shouted out aloud. 'Hurrah! It's working again. At last.' He held up the document with new wonder. *Who knows, perhaps this isn't just about Dachau. Perhaps Joachim found out something about the Nazis and Hitler that they don't want anyone to know.* The more he thought about it, the more sense it made. *That'll be why they put him in the camp in the first place. Can this document change everything?* He blinked. *Perhaps.* Julius felt new hope. *Yes would have been better, but perhaps is better than maybe. Probably.* An outrageous thought came to him. *Can I change the future?* The answer made him laugh with joy. *Yes.*

If I can only get this to the Manchester Guardian, then everything will be all right. They'll print it and whatever it says will be a real blow to Hitler. For all I know, that could be the end for him and his Nazis. And as Mussolini is much the same, he could be toppled too. Which would mean Lou won't have to marry her fascist. And then what will people think? They'll all be amazed at what I've done.

Now, finally, Julius understood. *That's why it kept saying maybe before. It all depends on what I do.* He felt a moment of unease, awed by his responsibility. *I just have to get it safely sent, and quickly too, as I imagine it needs to be published pretty soon if it's going to have a chance of stopping Lou's wedding. How long have I got? Ten days? It's too late to send it from here as the post offices will be closed by now. And anyway, it wouldn't be safe, as they might seize and open it.* The very thought made him queasy. *Venice then. I just hope I won't be searched at the frontier tomorrow.* He felt a strange, heady joy. *Everything will be good, everything will be perfect, I'm sure of it.*

Four

Early the next morning Karl appeared with a uniformed assistant and a large box. 'That's a lot of propaganda,' Claude grumbled. 'We'll have to rearrange all the suitcases.'

Poor Claude.

Despite these complaints, Karl made no effort to help, and he stood watching as his assistant, Frank and Maude removed and repacked the luggage, placing the box discreetly beneath other bags. But when it was done, he handed out rewards. 'A little token of Germany's gratitude.' He gave Claude a bottle of schnapps and offered everyone an enamel badge with a black swastika inside a red circle.

'I already have two,' said Maude, laughing, 'but I'll happily take a third.'

Frank couldn't hide his delight. 'Fantastic. I can wear it beside my BUF one.'

Karl gave him an indulgent smile. 'A nice idea, but I

wouldn't advise it today. The Austrians don't see the world as we do. At least not yet.'

Actually, it's probably good that we're taking Karl's Nazi papers. If the frontier guards see them, they won't be suspicious of us and they won't search me. Probably. A thought occurred to Julius. *Did you arrange all this, Predictor? Can you make things happen?* He blinked. *Perhaps.* Unclear though the answer was, it still warmed him.

They took their places in the car, which now had a new arrangement. With Sam gone and Claude driving, Lilian sat in the front and Julius found himself wedged between his half-siblings. *Oof, that was close. You're a lucky cyclist. And we were inches from that truck. I'd forgotten what an awful driver he is. You're right to keep hiding your eyes with your fingers, Mother. Oh, thank goodness – we're stopping.*

They pulled into a filling station and waited their turn for the attendant to set to work. 'What does that mean?' asked Frank, pointing at a large banner that read DEUTSCHLAND ERWACHE! DIE JUDEN KOMMEN!

'Germany grow up, the Jews are coming,' said Lilian.

'Mother, no,' Maude corrected her with a laugh. 'It's wake up, of course.'

'Though it doesn't look like they're coming but going,' said Frank, pointing. At the other petrol pump, a man in the dark suit and hat of Orthodox Jewry was waiting as the attendant refilled his small car, his family crowded inside and luggage tied precariously to the roof.

I wonder what's happened to them? Something pretty bad to make them leave like that.

Maude's eyes narrowed with disgust. 'Lots of them are slinking off these days,' she said. 'And good riddance.'

'Not to England, I hope,' said Frank.

'Tom's already on top of that,' said Claude. 'He's got a new campaign going. No to the refuge-Jews. Rather clever, I thought.'

How lovely.

They set off again. The day was fine and clear and the Alps were visible ahead, growing higher on the horizon as they drove. *Should I have put it in my pocket? But if we're searched, that's where they'd look first.* The road climbed more steeply and grew windier, they passed a lake, and the slopes on each side of the road pierced the tree line and then grew into rocky, snow-capped peaks. As they went through a small town of traditional painted houses, Julius saw a sign that read GRENZE. *Doesn't that mean frontier?* The car fell into a subdued silence. *I'm nervous about leaving Germany and they're nervous about going into Austria.*

But in the event, none of them needed to worry. They were waved through the German side with nothing more than a salute, a passport check and a stamp to the triptyque, while the only awkwardness on the Austrian side was self-inflicted. When the border official came to the car to ask for their passports, Claude and Lilian both shot out their arms and chanted, 'Heil Hitler.'

The frontier officer gave them a weary look. 'Not here, Englishman, not here.' The Austrian customs inspection was perfunctory and they were soon on their way.

'You see,' said Maude. 'I said it would be easy.'

The road grew windier as they climbed and descended among the peaks. 'You're going awfully fast,' said Lilian, with a nervous laugh.

'Sorry, Pet.'

Will that rotten-looking barn be repaired? Julius blinked. *Yes.* He felt himself smile. *It's definitely working again. So much for you, Other. You can't stop me now.* He glanced up at a bank of snow in surprise. *That looks almost like . . . It is. A swastika. So there are Nazis in Austria, too.* He felt a need to check. *Will Hitler be here, too?* He blinked. *Maybe.* This time the answer didn't trouble him. *Which means no, I'm sure, if I can only get this document in the post.*

At a spot where the view was especially striking, Claude pulled off the road and they got out of the car to look. 'Aren't you going to take a picture?' he asked.

'Oh yes.' Julius took out the Brownie from its bag. *It is beautiful, no denying.* He glanced down into the viewfinder and framed the picture, only to change his mind. *That's a much better shot. The four of them standing in a line by the car, in profile as they stare towards the view. Claude looking sneery, Frank bored, Mother enraptured and anxious, and Maude dreamy.* Click, went the shutter.

Frank was the one who noticed. 'Hey, you didn't give us any warning.'

I didn't know you were so vain. Julius took another with them all posing. *Only Maude looks just the same as before.*

'It's so enchanting here, so absolutely delightful,' said Lilian. 'The little fields with their fences, the beautiful houses, the cows with their tinkly bells, and that dear little church right up there on the hill. Doesn't it all make you think of those tiny little darlings floating about, playing and laughing?'

Oh no, not the fairies.

'Quite so, Pet,' said Claude blandly.

The fairies, the fairies. She hasn't mentioned them since I got out of the Mid-Wales. Though she had in a few of her letters, recounting how she was sure she'd seen them in the bottom of the garden. *Mosquitoes, probably, or bluebottles. Claude, for all your smiles, I know you're embarrassed. Frank's smirking. But Maude looks rather charmed. Shame on you, half-sister.*

They climbed back into the car. *What are you doing with Karl's box, Maude? Oh, that. Claude won't be pleased at all.*

'This is awfully interesting,' she said as they settled back onto the road. 'It says that Jesus was a fearless Aryan warrior who battled against evil Jewish priests.'

Will I work as a cameraman again? Do I dare ask? Julius decided he did, and blinked. *Yes.* He felt a joyous sense of relief. *Hurrah, hurrah. Everything's going to be all right.*

'What are you reading?' asked Claude warily.

'The Völkischer Beobachter, of course,' said Maude.

'You got one out of the box?'

I knew it.

'I need something to read to pass the time. And it's good practice for my German.'

'Well, just make damn sure that nobody sees,' said Claude.

Maude laughed. 'Stop being such an old woman, Pa. If any Austrian did see it, I'm sure he'd shake me by the hand. And anyway, we'll be in Italy soon.'

'Claude,' said Lilian in a warning voice. 'Too fast.'

'Sorry, Pet.'

Julius wondered if he dared ask, but then he did. *Will I see Linda again?* He blinked. *Yes.* He felt a joy. *Everything's going to be wonderful. Who knows, when people understand that I was the one who got Joachim's document to the Manchester Guardian, and got rid of Hitler and Mussolini, I may be famous.* He thought of the orderlies at the Mid-Wales, of Samson, the Reverend and Captain Williams, and of his friends at the film studio. *They'll all be amazed. And I bet that's why it said I'd see Linda again. I'll run into her at the studios, she'll have heard about all the things I've done and she'll be so surprised . . .*

'And it says only members of a genetically superior race can fly an aeroplane. The Wright Brothers were tall and had long skulls, large noses and blue eyes and were classic Aryans. Jews and other inferior races can hardly fly a kite, let alone an aeroplane.'

Who thinks up this nonsense? I can't believe anyone takes it seriously, but clearly some people do. Such as my family.

'Actually, that all fits in rather well with something I read recently by H. G. Wells,' said Claude, to confirm Julius' thought. 'He's got a new book out, The Shape of Things to Come, which is an absolute corker by the way, and which makes all kinds of fascinating predictions about the future. He says there'll be another war and everything will go completely to ruin, but then the world will be saved and put in good order by a band of tough but enlightened airmen. A sort of dictatorship of the noble. I rather see Frank as one of those chaps, flying about, giving commands, and putting the world to rights. What d'you say, Frank?'

Frank laughed awkwardly. 'I really don't know.'

You'd love that, of course you would. Bossing everybody around. Yes, it's there on your face.

'What d'you say, Pet?' said Claude. 'D'you see Frank as one of these dictator airmen chaps?'

'I don't see why not,' said Lilian with a half-laugh.

Will I . . . ?

Julius never finished his question because then, as they rounded a bend in the road, he saw that the windscreen was suddenly filled by a tractor, pulling a trailer stacked with logs. For an instant he saw the man driving the tractor – a huge figure, built like one of the trees he was hauling – raise his hand as if to try and push them back, then Julius heard a sharp squealing of brakes, and he just managed to put out his arms to save himself before he was thrown forwards into the wall of luggage. For what seemed like a surprisingly long time, he felt the car swerve to the right, to the left and then to the right again. *Perhaps we won't hit anything after all?* But then, at the very moment that this thought came to him, he felt himself pressed hard against suitcases and he heard a loud crash, a scraping of metal and tinkling of glass. A moment later the car was motionless, the engine was silent, and all was strangely still. *My right arm moves. My left arm too. Legs move. Hands and fingers move. Neck moves. Head feels all right. Arms a little sore where I hit the suitcases. Bit of a cut on the back of my hand but nothing worse than that. Frank looks fine, just startled, and Maude.* A disturbing thought came to him. *Why didn't it tell me? But then I never asked. I'm sure it would have if I had.* Then a darker thought came to him. *I wonder if it was the Other that made us crash?*

'Is anyone hurt?' asked Claude.

'I think we're just about all right back here,' said Julius.

'I've been worse,' said Lilian, 'though I can't for the life of me think when.'

'Poor Pet,' said Claude. 'That damn fool. He was coming right at me.'

'Claude,' said Lilian, a hardness in her voice, 'you were in the middle of the road. And I told you several times that you were driving much too fast.'

'Sorry, Pet,' said Claude.

Finally we see things exactly as they are. Mother's the boss and Claude has to swallow everything down.

Julius followed Frank out of the car and saw that, of all of them, Claude was in the worst state. He had a cut on his forehead and the handkerchief that he held to it was stained scarlet. Lilian, as she told them, had managed to shield herself against the dashboard just in time. Frank had a sore shoulder and slight cut to his arm, and Maude had hurt her knee, but that was all.

'Oh hell,' said Claude, looking at the front of the car.

Actually, I thought it would be worse. Julius saw, from its scraped trunk and missing branches, that the car had glancingly struck a tree by the roadside – a small one, that would have looked at home in somebody's sitting room covered with lights and topped with an angel. One headlamp had been torn off and lay in pieces in the road, the right mudguard was bent beyond recognition, as was the right part of the bumper, while the right front wheel was buckled and flat. Julius glanced round and saw that the tractor had stopped some distance further down the road, where the driver was checking the logs on his trailer. *If it was the Other, it didn't manage to do us that much damage.*

'And we have to be in Venice tomorrow to meet Harriet and Harold,' said Lilian. There was an ominous restraint in her voice.

It was only then that Julius realized. *What if I can't post Joachim's document? Perhaps that's what the Other was after?* He managed to calm himself. *No, it'll be fine, I'm sure. The Predictor said so.*

'The radiator seems all right, thank goodness,' said Claude, stooping down to look. 'So long as the front axle isn't buckled it won't be a disaster. Of course, we'll have to change the wheel.' He began fidgeting about the car. 'Where are the spanners?'

Nobody knew. But then help came from an unexpected

quarter. 'Oh look,' said Maude, glancing down the road. 'The chap you almost hit is coming over.'

He was striding purposefully towards them. *He really is quite a giant.*

'He doesn't look very happy,' said Maude.

'Maudie,' said Claude, 'can you tell him that I'm very sorry if I caused any trouble, and that I hope he's all right?'

Julius smiled. *Look at you – you're scared. For all your bluster, you're nothing but a big coward.*

But then, as he grew nearer, the man's face softened and he broke into a surprisingly high-pitched giggle.

Maude began talking to him. 'It's because of our GB sticker,' she explained, laughing too. 'He thinks it's absolutely hilarious because we're English, so of course we're always driving on the wrong side of the road.'

Julius felt a slight sense of disappointment. *Lucky Claude. So he won't knock you for six after all. Though he has every right, seeing as you almost killed him.* Instead, the farmer gave them a hand. Somehow, he knew where the spanners and the jack were kept, and in a moment the five of them had become embarrassed bystanders, awkwardly handing him tools as he ripped away the wrecked mudguard, which he told them to keep, and then changed the wheel. After that he had Claude try the engine, which started without trouble.

'He says there's a good mechanic in Innsbruck,' Maude translated, 'who should be able to fix the rest.'

'Ask him what I should give him for his trouble,' asked Claude, getting out his wallet. 'Though all I have is Reichsmarks, damn it.' But the farmer was already striding away, giving them a slow wave.

Claude's nervousness about the front axle proved groundless and the car carried them without incident to the mechanic. *It's a very small place.* Only a single car was visible in the yard: an ancient machine that looked pre-war, and which was clearly a source of scavenged parts, as it lacked three wheels and two doors. The mechanic peered at the Austin and scratched his head. 'He says it won't be easy,' Maude translated, 'especially the headlight, because people in Innsbruck don't have English cars, let alone new ones like this.'

New? The Austin's ten years old, at least.

'He says he could order one but it'll take several weeks.'

Lilian lost her temper. 'Several weeks?'

'I can try the RAC,' said Claude. 'They can send parts out in just a day or two. But of course tomorrow's Sunday, and Monday's Easter. Damn and damn.'

'Claude,' Lilian reminded him icily, 'we have to be in Venice tomorrow evening. I'm not going to miss meeting Harriet and Harold.'

Claude looks as if he'd be quite happy to dodge the Red couple.

But then Maude talked again to the mechanic and found that there was another possibility. 'He's being very kind. He says that he could finish it by tomorrow morning, even though that's Easter Sunday, probably around eleven, so long as we don't mind that it's not a perfect job. The spare wheel won't be an exact match with the others, nor the headlamp, but everything will work.'

'I'm not sure that's a good idea,' began Claude. 'I mean who knows . . .'

'Tell him that's fine,' said Lilian firmly.

'We're really going to have to dash tomorrow,' said Claude glumly. 'It's a long way to Venice.'

'Just be sure you dash very carefully,' said Lilian.

Oddly enough, it was only now that Julius realized what it all meant. *But this is good news – fantastic news. We'll have to stay here overnight, which means that I can post Joachim's document from here. Thank you, Predictor.*

The mechanic ordered a large taxi that took them and their luggage to a hotel, where the staff showed great concern at their injuries. Claude's eyes were fixed on Karl's box as it was placed on the luggage trolley. *How nervous you are, Stepfather. You're worried someone will open it and find stacks of the Völkischer Beobachter. Though what you should really be worrying about are Joachim's scribbled pages in my pocket.* He let his fingers brush over his jacket, feeling them there. *Like a bomb with a fuse. And to light it, all I have to do is get away from them all for a moment or two.*

Yet escaping the others did not prove easy. Though Julius only had a few scratches, Lilian insisted he go with them to a nearby chemist, where antiseptic ointment and bandages were applied, and afterwards he had to join them first for lunch and then for a walk around the town. *I'll never get free at this rate.* 'I wouldn't mind going back and taking a picture of that church,' he said finally. *Claude has that look – we can't have the family lunatic roaming free.*

'I'm sure there'll be lots of other nice churches you can take pictures of,' he said.

'I really liked that one.' *You can't very well stop me.* 'I'll see you back at the hotel, all right?'

'Don't be late,' said Lilian. 'We'll be leaving for dinner at seven, remember.'

Claude gave him a stern look. 'And . . .'

'I know, I know. No silliness. Don't worry.'

As if I would. I'm fine now. Never been better in all my life. Never been righter and brighter. Julius' first problem was the banks. *They all seem closed. Of course, it's Saturday. Damn.* Eventually he found a small bureau de change where he changed a ten-shilling note into Austrian money. *Shillings into Schillings*. Finding an envelope and buying stamps at the post office was easy enough, despite his lack of German, but that still left one other difficulty. *The address. I suppose I could write, 'The Manchester Guardian, Manchester, England' and it would probably get there.* He frowned. Probably didn't seem good enough for something so important. *I'll find a copy of the newspaper – it must have the address printed somewhere.*

Julius went from newspaper kiosk to newspaper kiosk, but though one had copies of The Times, and another had the Telegraph and the Daily Mail, the Manchester Guardian was nowhere to be seen. Finally, just as Julius was beginning to lose heart, a newspaper seller who had copies only of French and Swiss papers saw his frustration and told him, 'Bibliothek,' pointing down the street and then pointing a finger towards his watch.

Julius guessed his meaning. *I should go to the library, which is in that direction, as they'll have a copy. But I should go quickly as it closes soon.* Thanking the man, he hurried on. *No time to get lost now. I'll keep checking as I go.* 'Bibliothek?' he asked of a grey-haired, limping man – *looks like he was in the war* – who nodded and pointed in the direction Julius was going. 'Bibliothek?' he asked of a woman in a fur coat carrying a small dog. *Still good.* 'Bibliothek?' Julius found himself met with a puzzled stare.

'Julius? Julius Sewell? What on earth are you doing here?'

Now it was Julius who was staring, as he tried to recognize the familiar face. A name jumped into his head as if from nowhere – *Bob Prowse* – and then a persona attached itself to the name. Bob Prowse, likeable, reliable Bob Prowse, who had worked as Julius' assistant cameraman on Waltzing in Warsaw. Julius recalled the question he had been asked. 'Actually, I'm on my way to a wedding. My sister's getting married in Rome.'

'Very nice.'

That awkward smile. 'How about you?'

'I'm skiing. Or I have been. I'm here with my brother and sister-in-law. They're off shopping for souvenirs. We're getting the sleeper train home tonight. More's the pity. Back to the grindstone.'

He's worried that I'll suggest we go for a cup of coffee and then start telling him about my madness, and how I jabbed into my gut with a penknife. You don't need to worry. 'Well, very good to run into you like this, Bob. I mean, what's the chance of that?' *Yes, he's smiling now.*

'Quite so. If it was in a picture, nobody'd buy it for a moment.'

I should go, too, but actually: 'One thing, though. I never did see Waltzing in Warsaw. How did it turn out?' *Oh good, he's still smiling.*

'Excellent, really excellent. It had a good run in the cinemas and did really well. In fact they've made another, Waltzing in Vilnius.'

'And the camerawork?'

'It was perfect. Especially that part that you were worried about. The banquet scene. It looked great. A lot of people said so and Bernstein was very pleased. No really, Julius, you did well.'

See, even though he's uneasy at meeting me, he still wants to raise my spirits with some good news. People want to be kind. Mostly, anyway. An odd thought came to him. *It must take a lot of work to make them cruel.* He thought of Lieutenant Hoffmann walking beside him in Dachau, prisoners flinching away from him. *He could have been anybody – somebody at a ticket kiosk in an underground station, or counting out coins and notes in a bank. I wonder what they had to do to make him what he is? What bribes and threats they had to use?*

Bob took a step back, about to say his goodbyes, but another question had come to Julius. *I shouldn't, but then . . .* 'One last thing and then I really must go. I don't suppose you know what Linda's up to these days?' *He looks startled. Hell.*

'You didn't hear? She got married a few months ago.'

I don't understand. Julius managed a smile. 'Wonderful. Who to?'

'Tony Clark. You remember? The assistant lighting man.'

'Well, that's great news. I'm very happy for her.'

'Anyway, I'd probably best be off. Find the souvenir hunters before we miss our train.' Bob Prowse broke into an awkward smile. 'See you around, old man.'

'Yes, see you around.' *It said we'd be married. Unless that was the Other.* Julius hurried on towards the library. *Just get it done, just get it done.* But when he got there, he saw people were straggling out of the door and one of the staff was blocking the way. 'Bibliothek?' asked Julius.

'Geschlossen.'

I can guess what that means. 'It'll only take a moment or two. A couple of minutes. It's very important.'

'Geschlossen.'

Damn, damn. If I'd only been here a little earlier. If only I hadn't met Bob. If only I hadn't stood talking for so long. If only I hadn't asked about Linda and Waltzing in Warsaw. Was it the Other who sent Bob? And I fell for it! He walked into a nearby park and slumped onto a bench. *Don't give in. There's too much at stake. Nothing's lost. The library opens at nine and it's not far from the hotel. With a bit of luck, I'll be able to hurry out after breakfast and get the address.* He made himself slow down and think through what had happened. *And the Predictor never lied. You didn't ask if you'd marry her, remember, but only if you'd see her again. And it said you'll be back working in pictures, so of course you'll see her every pay day.* He tried to fight down a feeling of resentment. *Tony Clark. He's a good man. How very like you, Linda. With your pretty looks, you might have got one of the studio high-ups but no, you picked an ordinary, unambitious but very decent man. He'll give you the happiness you deserve. I'm glad for you.*

He found himself thinking, of all things, of the hatch between the kitchen and dining room at her parents' house, where he'd gone to dinner a handful of times. *I always liked it there. I felt calm.* Linda's father was an electrician who occasionally worked at the studios and both he and his wife had been in awe of Julius. *Because I had a posh accent and came from a rich family. Though her father was worth twenty of them or me. I tried to make him see it, but he couldn't.* He had been in the trenches for much of the war and had been wounded twice. *I saw the way he grimaced when he got up from the dining table. And all through it he had a wife and tiny daughter to worry about. His wife saw him come home, torn to pieces, saw him recover, and then watched him go back for more.*

Now he remembered. *That's why I thought of the hatch.* When he'd first mentioned Linda to his parents and he had answered their many questions about where she lived and what work her father did, Claude had broken into a knowing smile. 'Let me guess,' he said, with a laugh, 'they have a hatch.' *Amusement at predictable poor taste. No, you're much better off with Tony Clark, Linda. I'm sure he has nice, kind parents. Mine would have ground you down and made you feel small about yourself.* And then, almost to his own surprise, he managed to retrieve his earlier good spirits. *You have a task, remember? Something which can change everything. That's all that matters.*

The next morning, soon after dawn, Julius was woken by the sound of Frank getting up and bustling about the room, fussing with his things. Julius glanced at his watch. *Six-thirty? You're very early. Rather you than me.* Allowing himself another half-hour's sleep, he went down to the breakfast room where he found only his mother. *Look at you – cake for breakfast? Well, why not?* When he asked where the others were, she had no idea. *As if it matters. Actually it's better, much better, as it means I can slip out without Claude making a fuss.* But hardly had Julius assembled a bread roll with cheese and ham when he saw Claude, Maude and Frank marching into the room. Claude looked furious, Maude bemused and Frank miserable, as if he wished the earth might swallow him up. *What have you done, Frank? And Claude has his, 'I wasn't a major in the army for nothing,' face.*

'There's no time for breakfast, I'm afraid,' he murmured dramatically. 'We have to leave straight away. And by straight away, I mean now, right this very moment.'

No.

'For goodness' sake, Claude,' said Lilian. 'I've just sat down to breakfast.'

Not entirely true. From the crumbs and plates I'd say that's your third piece of cake.

'And where do we have to go?'

'To the garage, of course,' Claude answered.

That makes no sense. 'But the car won't be ready yet,' said Julius.

'It doesn't matter. The important thing is that we leave the hotel right away. Immediately.'

Julius took a large bite from his roll.

'I'm sure nothing will happen,' said Maude languidly. 'And I'd rather like some breakfast.'

'Sorry, Maude, but we just can't take that chance.'

'I'm really sorry,' moaned Frank.

What on earth did you do? Piss on the Austrian flag? 'I have to go out just for a moment,' said Julius. 'There's another picture I want to take. It won't take a second and I'm all packed up and ready to go.' *Oh no, the staring eyes.*

'Absolutely out of the question,' Claude hissed.

Damn, damn. Julius struggled against a sense of defeat.

Why did I have to stop and talk to Bob? It's like it was testing me and I failed. He tried to hold himself together. *This is no time to weaken.* He brushed his hand over his jacket, feeling the faint presence of Joachim's document in his pocket. *I can post it from Venice tomorrow morning, so there'll only be one day lost.* Doubts crept back. *Assuming we can get there tonight, that is. And assuming that that one day doesn't make all the difference.* He tried to ponder the uncertainties before him – how long the post would take, how long the Manchester Guardian would need to have the document translated into English, how long the world would need to take notice. *How many days till Louisa's wedding? Nine.* Possibilities seemed to slither about him. *Damn, damn. Don't lose heart. There must be a way. The Predictor said so. But I was so close. If I'd reached the library three minutes earlier, I bet I could have found a paper and scribbled down the address.*

In the taxi driving back to the mechanic, Julius finally learned the cause of Claude's panic. 'I have to say I'm quite annoyed with Karl,' he declared, twisting round from the passenger seat to face the others and keeping his voice low. 'I said it was a bad idea, taking all that nonsense of his. A damned stupid idea.'

'That's not fair,' insisted Maude. 'We were almost home and dry, till . . .'

'It was so heavy,' Frank interrupted miserably.

It emerged that the three of them had gone to the address Karl had given them, which they had found without difficulty, but when they went up to the apartment, which was on the fourth floor, Frank had tripped and dropped the box. It fell open and dozens of copies of Völkischer Beobachter cascaded down the stairs.

No wonder you look like the puppy that's crapped on the rug.

'The Nazi chap was waiting for us with his door open,' Claude explained, 'and he gave me a very nasty look, which I didn't think was fair at all, seeing as we'd taken a big risk bringing the stuff across the frontier.' Even with the Nazi's help it had taken them time to gather up the copies back into the box, and all the while people were going by. 'The first was a young chap who didn't seem too interested, fortunately,' said Claude, 'in fact he gave me a little smile. But just after him came an elderly woman who looked very disapproving and who said something.'

'Don't you know the Völkischer Beobachter's illegal in Austria?' remembered Maude helpfully.

Frank finally felt a need to defend himself. 'Nobody offered to lend me a hand. And like I said, it was so heavy.'

'If you'd only asked, I'd have helped you,' said Maude. 'I just hope we haven't got that poor fellow into hot water.'

'I'm more concerned about us right now,' said Claude,

lowering his voice further. 'What if the police contact the frontier people and have us stopped?'

For once Julius found himself in agreement with his stepfather. *That's all I need – to be stuck in an Austrian jail.*

They reached the garage yard, where the mechanic greeted them with the cheerful smile of one who knows he has done well. 'Good news,' Maude translated. 'He says he's just finished the job. He was here till nine last night working, as the problems were very difficult, but with patience he was able to find all the right solutions.'

See? Perhaps it'll all be fine after all.

'Do thank him,' said Claude.

When they walked into the repair room, Julius' heart sank. *Claude will explode and then we'll never get out of here. It'll be like that time when he sued the man who mended the garden fence.* Unlike the other wheels, which had sturdy hubs, the new spare had a web of thin spokes so it looked as if it should rightly be attached to a very plump bicycle. The front bumper and the mudguard had been neatly bashed back into shape but their black paint didn't match – it looked brown compared to the rest and was matt rather than glossy. Most striking, though, was the new headlamp. Julius glanced round at the scavenged car in the yard. *Of course, that's where it came from. It only has one left now.* It was brass-coloured, tall and square, and resembled the kind of lamp that might be seen in an old painting, carried by a watchman on the end of a long pole. The mechanic had welded on a narrow shelf for it to rest on, between the radiator and the wheel cover. He turned on the engine and proudly switched the lights on and off several times. *Don't look so pleased.*

Lilian had her eyes half closed, Frank looked shocked and Maude was struggling not to laugh. As for Claude, he stared for a moment, his mouth slightly open.

Why aren't you shouting?

'Don't worry, Pet,' Claude said at last, in a low voice. 'When we get back to Kingston, I'll have the chaps at the garage set to work on it. It'll look as good as new, I promise.'

'Let's hope so,' said Lilian in a clipped voice.

Fear beats rage. You really are a big coward. Well, so much the better. All that matters is that we get away from here.

They soon did. Lilian paid, they loaded up the luggage and then set out onto the road. *What's that odd sound, like a wind blowing? I hope nothing's wrong with the car? Of course, it's just the air passing round the new lamp.*

They began climbing steeply along a winding, switchback road. 'I warned you about going too fast,' said Lilian.

'It's a long way to Venice,' said Claude. 'We have to keep moving if we're going to have a chance of getting there tonight.'

Quite so. 'And it's not a bad stretch of road,' Julius said. 'It's very open so you can see that there's nothing coming the other way.'

'We should just be glad the Brenner's open,' said Claude. 'We're lucky. The chap at the hotel said it was shut fast with snow just a week ago. If it still was, we'd have a hell of a detour.'

Thank you, Predictor.

They climbed steadily higher, passing forest, then grassy slopes, until finally they reached a bleak, stony landscape with deep piles of dirty snow on either side of the road. A sign by the roadside read GRENZE.

'Nobody say a word here,' said Claude dramatically, as they approached the frontier. 'You hear me, Julius?'

Why me? I wasn't the one who threw Nazi newspapers down the stairs of the Austrian apartment block.

But again, Claude had no need to worry. At the Austrian frontier post their documents were checked, the triptyque stamped and they were waved on with hardly a glance. 'Hurrah,' shouted out Frank as they drove on.

'I said it was nothing to worry about,' said Maude languidly. 'We could have enjoyed our breakfast.'

'Who's to know what might have happened if we'd set out five minutes later?' Claude insisted.

No delay. That's good. But the Italian side was slow. *That damn lamp*. The passport official just smiled, but the customs man was so amused that he called over two colleagues to see. *As they think it's so funny, with luck they'll leave us be.* But they then conducted a very thorough search of the luggage, showing particular interest in Lilian's pearls, asking where they had been bought and for how much, though in the end no duty was charged.

'Damned unprofessional, all that sniggering and smirking,' said Claude when they finally drove on. 'Just because we had a little prang.'

Maude agreed. 'I don't know how they can call themselves fascists. And they didn't say a thing when they gave their salute, there was no heil Mussolini or whatever that would be in Italian. They didn't even click their heels.' She pointed at a huge poster of Mussolini wearing a uniform and helmet. 'To be honest I don't know why they make such a fuss of him. Hitler's so much better-looking.'

Claude felt she had gone too far. 'It's what he does, Maudie. It's his tremendous dynamism.'

Frank had other concerns. 'I don't believe it,' he said miserably, searching through his pockets. 'I think I left my swastika badge behind. I had it on my bedside table at the hotel, and then we were in such a rush to leave . . .'

'Poor Frank,' said his mother. 'Maude, why don't you give him one of yours, as you've got three.'

'It's not my fault if he can't take care of his things,' said Maude sniffily.

'Maude,' said her mother in a warning voice.

It's as if I've jumped back ten years. Julius reached into his pocket. 'Here, you can have mine.' *I really don't want it.*

'Isn't that kind?' said Lilian.

You don't look keen but you'll take it anyway. There – you're rubbing it on your shirt tail to clean off the lunacy. Julius watched as they sped round a hairpin bend. *Will we reach Venice tonight?* There was no answer, nothing at all. *It's like the Other can stop it from working sometimes, like a radio being jammed.*

Before long they reached a wider valley, the road became less winding and Claude was able to put on more speed. The road was untarmacked and a routine soon developed. Peering over the luggage, Julius would see in the distance what looked like a black dot in a halo of billowing beige. This would grow steadily larger till Claude shouted, 'Close windows,' and then Maude and Frank, who liked to have theirs open a little, hurriedly wound them shut. A moment later Claude slammed on the brakes, a car sped past, and they became lost in a thick cloud of dust, after which they crept along at a snail's pace till it cleared. *Damn, here comes another. They slow us down so.*

Everyone settled into the journey as best they could.

Lilian had a book to read and Frank and Maude began playing Slimers across Julius' lap. *They didn't ask me to join in. Though I wouldn't want to, anyway. Damn it, there's another car coming.*

'Close windows,' commanded Claude.

'These roads are just awful,' Maude complained. 'They're much better in Germany. And I haven't seen a single proper petrol pump yet. It's so primitive here, selling it in those big tin cans.'

At least they're selling it, even though it's Easter Sunday. The last thing we need is to run out of petrol. Julius distracted himself by glancing through the window and counting Mussolinis. *There's hardly a wall without him.* Here he was in half a dozen posters, grimly staring out from beneath a helmet, his arm raised in the Roman salute. *Eleven.* Here he was in a civilian suit, eyes impassioned and mouth open as he made a speech. *Twelve.* Here, unexpectedly, were two Mussolinis frowning with emotion as they played the violin. *Fourteen.* Here were four more athletically leaping over obstacles. *Eighteen.* Here, pasted to the side of a church, were three, each planting a tree. Julius touched his jacket. *Will it win? Will it beat them all?* Again, silence. *Damn.* A range of strange, spiky peaks came into view ahead, that Claude said were the Dolomites. *They look so odd, like some invented landscape in a painting.*

Everyone was getting hungry. 'There's somewhere to eat,' said Maude, pointing.

Claude sped on. 'I think we can do better than that. It looked like a real workman's place.' He gave a little laugh. 'Just the ticket for Harriet and Harold.'

'But they're all like that round here,' Maude complained. 'And I didn't get any breakfast, remember.'

A sit-down lunch will take ages. 'We could find some bread and cheese at a shop and eat it as we drive on?' Julius suggested.

Lilian wasn't keen. 'That hardly sounds like a proper meal. And the crumbs will go everywhere.'

I thought you wanted to get to Venice tonight.

Reluctantly, Claude agreed to stop at the next town they came to, and before long a tall church steeple came into sight ahead of them. 'There'll probably be somewhere here,' Claude grumbled.

As they drew towards the centre of the little town Julius heard barking and Frank wound down his window. 'It's a little black dog,' he said, amused. 'He's chasing the car.'

'There's a place,' said Maude, pointing.

'Where?' asked Claude, looking round.

'Over there on the right.'

It was at that same moment that a cyclist flitted into their path from a side road. Claude swerved and Julius heard a noise from Frank's side of the car, a kind of thump. The barking stopped. *Oh God. But don't stop. We can't.*

'What was that?' said Maude suspiciously.

'Nothing, probably,' said Claude.

Thank goodness, he's kept going.

Frank was peering back out from his window. 'I think we hit him.'

'Stop!' screamed Maude.

'I rather think we should,' agreed Lilian.

Damn, he's slowing down. The money has spoken.

As they drew to a halt, Claude turned to face his wife and Maude. 'Pet, Maudie, I do think . . .' But he got no further because Maude opened her door, climbed out and began striding back down the road. Now everybody was getting out. Julius could make out a small black shape lying still by the roadside.

Poor little thing.

'Maudie, wait,' Claude called out, but she took no notice. Lilian began hurrying after her and then they all were.

Julius saw the shutters of a house swing open, he glimpsed a head with curly grey hair poke out, and then a loud wailing filled the air. *Oh God.*

'I knew we should've kept going,' murmured Claude. 'It's not as if there's anything we can do. And now it's all turning into a damned silly mess.' The wailing acted like the tolling of a bell and people were drifting out of houses and shops to see what was happening.

Maude crouched down to look at the dog. 'He's breathing,' she called out, triumphant.

In a moment Julius was close enough to see for himself. The animal, which lay motionless on the ground, was bleeding a little from his side and his head. *He looks a nice sort of dog. Poor creature. His head doesn't look too good. For that matter, nor does this crowd.* Several dozen people were now gathered around them and Julius sensed they were of two minds. Some shot the foreigners angry looks, but others – seemingly the majority – appeared more curious than angry. *At least that woman's stopped wailing.* Yet the respite proved short-lived. Julius glanced at the window where she had been, now empty, but then the door beneath opened and out she came, crying out louder than ever, 'Mio cagnolino, mio povero cagnolino.' Shooting the foreigners a furious glare, she scooped up the dog in her arms, cradling him like an infant.

'Ce n'était guère de ma faute,' insisted Claude. 'Le chien a déboulé devant la voiture.'

For once I agree. It really wasn't his fault.

Julius hadn't expected anyone to understand Claude's French, but some seemed to sense what he had meant. 'Il cane è pazzo,' said one with a shrug. 'Pazzo,' agreed another.

'Poor little Pazzo,' said Maude, reaching out to stroke his head, only for the grey-haired woman to twist away so she couldn't reach.

'Y a-t-il un vétérinaire en ces lieux?' Claude asked the woman.

Now he'll get out the wallet. Yes, I knew it.

'J'insiste pour payer.' He was answered with what sounded like a torrent of curses.

Oh hell. And here's worse trouble. Two figures in uniform were making their way through the crowd. *Are they police? Their uniforms look more military. Some kind of fascists, probably. Are you going to arrest Claude? Any other time I'd be delighted, but not today.*

It was not to be. With the help of an English-speaker, who had appeared together with the two in uniform, Claude managed to recount his version of the accident, which, once he had been found in a nearby bar, was corroborated by the cyclist. Seeing that no crime had been committed, the men in uniform, whose interest in the matter had never been strong, told Claude that he was free to go.

'But we can't just leave Pazzo like this,' said Maude. 'You said you were going to fetch a vet.'

Poor Claude. You thought you were getting off scot-free.

'Of course,' said Claude stiffly, and he turned to the English-speaker. 'Can you take us to a vet here? I'll pay, of course.' Some among the crowd, which had been dispersing, now returned, seeing that something else of curiosity might happen, and one asked the English-speaker to translate Claude's words, which were met with approving nods.

I hope this vet's nearby. But he was nothing of the sort. The English-speaker explained that there was none to be found in the town and the nearest was some kilometres away back along the road they had just come down, while he usually dealt with cows and horses.

We can't go back. Oh good, Claude's got out his wallet again.

Explaining that they were in a great hurry as he had an important appointment in Venice, he offered to pay the woman to take her dog to the vet, only for the English-speaker to lower his voice. 'As you like, but you should know that he isn't her dog. He lives on the street and belongs to nobody. She just feeds him sometimes. And you should also know that if you leave money, it won't go to the vet or the dog.' He glanced towards the woman. 'She spends every lira on wine.'

Then there's no use.

Claude was about to reply but Maude was quicker. 'If we can't go back to the last town,' she said, 'then we'll just have to take Pazzo with us to Venice.'

'Maudie, really,' said Claude.

Actually, why not? Good idea, Maude.

'There'll be plenty of vets there,' she insisted, 'and not just for horses and cows. And then when he's better, we can bring him back here. We'll have to come through this way to get to Munich.'

Claude looked like he was about to disagree, but the English-speaker had again been asked to translate, and Maude's words were met with a cheer from the crowd, and even the wailing woman gave a smile. She handed the dog to Julius.

Why me? Maude looks quite annoyed she didn't give him to her. But at least we haven't been lynched and can go. So well done, half-sister.

The English-speaker had one last truth for them. 'But he's not called Pazzo. He has no name except Dog. Pazzo means mad, crazy.'

'He's definitely Julius' then,' said Frank, causing the others to smile.

We'll see who's laughing when Hitler and Mussolini are gone, and Louisa's been rescued from the fascist you all adore so much. Julius carried him over to a nearby street fountain to give his wounds a clean. *Actually, you don't look that bad. Though I wish you'd wake up.*

'And we will take him to a vet in Venice, won't we?' demanded Maude as they walked on.

Lilian gave Claude a testing look.

'Yes, yes, of course,' he answered impatiently. 'And we'll do whatever he says we should.'

Put you to sleep, kill you off, or so he hopes. Poor little beast.

Claude wanted them to leave the dog in the car while they had lunch, but Maude, Lilian and Julius all insisted that he must come with them to the restaurant. This was precisely the sort of place that Claude had been keen to avoid: a large, plain-walled osteria that was crowded with people in work clothes, speaking loudly. *It smells good. Will they object to a dog? Nobody seems to mind. And look, some of them are applauding us. From villains to heroes. Claude's giving them a superior smile. Who'd have guessed you wanted to drive on and leave him there?* Julius felt a twinge of guilt. *Then so did I. Sorry, Pazzo.*

'I'll take him now,' said Maude.

All right, all right.

Julius handed the limp animal to her as Claude, in his curious French, managed to explain to the waiter that they were in a hurry, and was told, 'Lasagne'. They all agreed, lasagne for everyone, and were led to a table, where Maude and Frank began devouring the bread. As Julius chewed on a piece, he sensed a hush in the restaurant and, glancing up, he felt a strange sense of recognition. A large, clumsy-looking man had walked in through the door together with a tiny woman twice his age, who looked about her with an air of defiance.

Look at their faces. Though she's tiny and he's huge, they're definitely mother and son. The son was carrying a large cardboard box, which he held with great care, but what Julius most noticed about him was the look in his eyes, which was a curious mixture of things: sly, knowing, furtive and anxious all at once. *I know you. You could be in the Mid-Wales. Yes, it's there in the glances that everyone's giving you.* Some seemed amused, others scowled. Julius watched uneasily as the pair sat at the table next to theirs, and he had a momentary sense of being in another place and time – the dining hall, keeping his eyes peeled, watching for trouble. The mother ordered for them both in a sharp, high-pitched voice and then the son reached over to the cardboard box, which he had put on a chair, only for his mother to stop him with a quick squeal of words. *What have you got in there? What is it you want to do? Something you shouldn't, clearly.* Julius tried to imagine what it might be like being this man in a small town of this kind. *Whatever it is you want to do, please don't. Make your life easier. Hurry up, lasagne.*

There was no sign of it. The waiter appeared and asked if they wanted any water or wine, causing Claude to prevaricate. 'I'm sure it's ghastly,' he murmured.

And I'm sure the waiter can guess what you just said.

Claude ordered a carafe of red, which soon appeared. 'I suppose it could be worse,' he declared, taking a large sip.

'Look,' said Maude excitedly. 'Pazzo's coming round.'

Julius saw the dog had opened his eyes. He looked about him, got to his feet on Maude's lap, wobbled unsteadily for a moment and then, abruptly, he jumped onto Julius'.

Hello.

'You silly,' said Maude, reaching to take him back, but Pazzo pulled away from her, growling. 'All right, all right, have it your own way,' she said crossly.

At least somebody round here likes me. As Julius began stroking the dog's head and it leaned in towards him, he became aware of a sudden movement from the table beside theirs and, looking up, he saw that sitting between the empty plates was a large black and white rabbit. *So that's what was in the box. I hope Pazzo doesn't think it's food. No, he's much too groggy. I don't see why the mother's so worked up, as it's only a rabbit.* She had got to her feet, though she was so tiny that she seemed barely taller than before, and began angrily berating her son. *You must've known he'd do this, so why did you let him bring it here? Unless it was more trouble to try and stop him?*

The other members of Julius' family had finally noticed.

'Oh look,' said Maude in delight. 'That man's got a big bunny.'

Now the mother tried to grab it, presumably to put it back in the box, but she had no chance, as her son leaned forwards and guarded it protectively with his arms. *He's done all this before. I still don't see why she's so bothered. Nobody here minded us bringing Pazzo.*

But then, with a look of wicked delight, the son got to his feet, lightly pushing his mother so she fell back into her chair and, his eyes twinkling with intent, he released the rabbit and called out in a loud voice, 'Vai, Mussolini, vai.'

What does that mean? Go, Mussolini, go?

It seemed ludicrous and yet the restaurant fell into a strained silence – all except for Julius' table. Maude was in peals of laughter. 'His bunny's called Mussolini,' she said. Frank was sniggering and both Claude and Lilian broke into deep, unrestrained guffaws.

'I don't think we should be laughing,' Julius began, only for Maude to roll her eyes.

Something bad will happen, I just know it.

As if in answer to Julius' thought, a small man with a sour expression, who Julius had noticed glowering at the mother and son when they first arrived, got up from his table and began shouting and jabbing his finger towards the son. Julius expected the mother to shout back, but instead she bowed her head and her reply was a beseeching bleat. The son, too, had lost his sly look and seemed panicked, hurriedly scooping the rabbit back into its box. *You're scared of him. I wonder who he is? Oh hell.*

The man was now stepping towards their own table and his jabbing finger was pointing at Claude and Maude. Though Julius couldn't understand a word that he said, he could guess. *Our leader insulted and made to look foolish in front of foreigners. I knew they shouldn't have laughed.*

'What on earth does this little fellow think he's up to?' said Claude grumpily.

But the man was already walking away, angrily declaiming as he went. *No.* As Julius had guessed he would, the man made his way to a table with two uniformed figures. *They're different from the ones who were in the crowd outside after we hit poor Pazzo. These look like police.* For a moment there was a tussle of wills, as the police waved their hands dismissively. *They can't be bothered with any of this. Oh good.* But the short man persevered, his voice growing louder and more agitated, till finally, with reluctance, the policemen got to their feet and walked over to the mother and son. Across the restaurant, the hum of chatter and the clink of cutlery had ceased, as everyone watched.

It's like a court scene in the pictures. The little denouncer was the prosecutor, the mother was the defence, pleading in a shrill voice, and the two policemen were the jury. *Just let him go. Why doesn't anyone else speak up? Some of them look like they want to. I suppose they're scared.* He could see who was winning, and eventually the police pulled the son to his feet. *Don't struggle – you'll just make it worse.* But he was docile and let himself be led from the restaurant, the mother hurrying behind them with the rabbit in the box, wailing as she went.

I saw something like this somewhere else. Julius struggled to remember. *The van in Frankfurt.* A few of the diners were smiling, but most were grimly silent. *They'd like to speak up but they don't dare. What will happen to him? Perhaps it won't be as bad as you think. They'll give him a warning and let him go.* But he found it hard to believe, as the irritable looks of the policemen, and the undisguised disgust with which they had regarded the son, all said otherwise. *It was only because he called the rabbit Mussolini. Nothing else.* But he knew that wasn't so. *No, it was because he was . . .* Even in his own thoughts, Julius found he had trouble with the word, though he'd thought it and said it enough times before now. *Not right in the head. Is that what they do here to people like . . .* With difficulty he managed to calm himself. *Not to foreigners. The Predictor promised everything would be all right. And I'm fine.*

'That seemed a bit strong,' said Lilian.

'People have to show respect,' said Claude soberly. 'It's important.'

'He looked nuts to me,' said Frank simply, and then, realizing what he had said, he glanced at Julius, smirking and watching for his reaction.

'It wouldn't have happened in Germany,' said Maude dreamily. 'Hitler loves animals.'

Don't you see that it was your own doing because you all laughed? No, there's no guilt or shame, nothing at all. Julius began asking the Predictor, *will he be all right?* only to change his mind. *He will, he'll be all right,* he told himself, without much conviction. Their lasagne finally arrived and they silently ate. Hungry though he was, Julius ignored the disapproving looks of Claude and Lilian, and gave a part of his portion to Pazzo, who enthusiastically gulped it down.

'I'd be careful with him,' Claude warned. 'He's a stray, remember. For all we know, he may be quite savage. And they have rabies here, don't forget.'

Quite as if he'd understood, Pazzo reached up and licked Julius' face. 'I'm not worried,' said Julius. 'And if I do get rabies, I promise not to bite any of you.' *Though it's what you all deserve.*

As they walked back to the car, Maude again tried to claim Pazzo but with no more success than before. 'As if I care,' she declared crossly. Pazzo's choice brought about a brief discussion between her and her brother, as they realized it would be impossible to play Slimers over the dog's head, and they agreed that Frank should sit in the middle seat. *So much for your carsickness. I finally get a proper view. Thank you, Pazzo. And what a view it is. Though I do wish the roads were less windy and a little faster.* Several times they climbed to a high pass and then descended along endless hairpin bends. The journey seemed cursed with delays and after an hour's driving they found themselves stopped for no clear reason in open country. *The houses all look very new here.*

Julius soon discovered why. Maude talked to a man on a bicycle who spoke German. 'They've found an unexploded shell just by the roadside,' she explained.

So this where the Italians fought the Austrians. Not the easiest spot. We're right up in the mountains. They heard a loud boom and the traffic jam moved on.

'D'you think we'll be there in time for dinner?' asked Lilian as dusk began to fall.

'I'm afraid not, Pet,' said Claude. 'We've still got a long way to go. If you're tired, we can always look for a place to stay somewhere round here.'

Please no.

Julius found he had an ally in his mother. 'Certainly not. We must get there today, however late we are, as Harriet and Harold will want to join us for breakfast at the hotel. I just hope they won't be worried to death about us not arriving tonight.' For dinner, this time with no complaints from Lilian, they made do with bread and cheese bought from a shop in a small town, which they ate while driving. Finally they reached the flat of the Po Valley, where Claude was able to get up to a good speed, though again they had to stop – twice – when the radiator overheated and they had to let the engine cool. Julius dozed off and when he woke he was surprised to see the moon shining on water. 'Where are we?' he asked.

'On the new causeway road to Venice,' said Claude. 'It was opened just last year. Another example of Mussolini's dynamic leadership.'

'And how long has he been leader of Italy?' asked Maude. 'A dozen years? Hitler would have finished this ages ago.'

'I don't think that's quite fair,' said Claude, but he didn't have the chance to elaborate, as they had come to the entrance of a car park.

There'll be nobody here at this hour. But, surprisingly, the kiosk at the entrance contained a bleary-looking figure who wrote out a chit for them and asked if they wanted transport. They waited half an hour in the cool night air till two gondolas appeared, one plain and functional for their luggage, and the other more elegant, with crimson seats for the passengers. Julius snapped a picture of his mother getting aboard, firmly grasping the hand of the gondolier, her face a curious mixture of feigned delight and panic. *It probably won't come out at all, as it's so dark.* Pazzo took to boat travel with surprising calm, allowing Julius to carry him aboard and settling comfortably into his lap.

Julius looked about him as they glided down narrow canals. *I've seen plenty of pictures but I never imagined it would be like this. It's so different when you're on the water looking up. I've never seen anywhere so beautiful. Though it'd be hard to capture. So much is in the rocking, the smell of seawater, the moonlight on the buildings.* He smiled to himself. *Nothing will go wrong now. How can it, in a place that's as lovely as this.* As Pazzo reached up and licked his chin, a thought came to him. *What if it's not just chance that he's here? What if the Predictor sent him to help me?* He stroked the dog's head. *Yes, you're on my side all right.*

Five

At breakfast the next morning, Julius bit into what he thought was a croissant but tasted unexpectedly sweet – *some Italian thing* – and listened as his mother listed churches she wanted to visit. *What excuse can I give them? I want to take some photos? But I could do that with them. I want to buy a souvenir? But who for? My friends back in the Mid-Wales? They'd never believe that. Linda?* Into his thoughts, quite unasked for, came a remembrance of when, light-headed from loss of blood and still digging away with his penknife, trying not to feel the pain, he glanced up and saw her looking round the door to his room, her eyes widening. *No, not Linda. Not even as an excuse.*

'I don't know why they can't make a hot breakfast in these Continental countries,' grumbled Claude. 'Has nobody taught them how to boil an egg and fry a bit of bacon?'

You're still sour from last night. First there had been the business at the hotel. When they had finally arrived, the tired-looking man at the front desk had glanced at Pazzo and then told them, apologetically, that pets were not permitted, and no amount of wheedling and indignation from Claude could change his mind. *And then my stepfather wanted to leave you out on the street.* Julius stroked Pazzo's head. *But nobody else was having that.*

The desk manager had rung another hotel not far away that was known for its tolerance of animals, and which happily had rooms, but, though the crisis had been resolved, Claude was then presented with a new reason for resentment. The porters loaded their luggage onto a trolley and they were all about to set out when Lilian realized she should leave a note for Harriet and Harold to explain their move, only to find herself handed one from them.

'They'll have been worrying to death where we've got to,' she said, shooting a look at Claude, the cause of their delay. But Harriet's note, which had evidently been left much earlier in the evening, instead offered apologies, at least of a kind. 'So sorry Ma and Pa and dearest everyone,' Lilian read. 'But H and I can't join you for dinner after all as something's come up. But see you tomorrow. We'll pop over in time for lunch. Can't wait. Love to all.'

'Something's come up?' said Claude, exasperated. 'And to think we raced here all the way from Innsbruck to meet them.'

'They're probably off meeting Bolshies,' said Maude with a smirk.

The second hotel, though it was a little dingier than the first, more than lived up to its reputation. Seeing the dried blood on Pazzo's head, the man at the desk insisted on calling a vet, despite the lateness of the hour and Claude's claims that it was unnecessary. *He just didn't want to pay up.* The vet had appeared with surprising rapidity, cleaned Pazzo's cuts, applied antiseptic and declared that he should be fine. *Which Claude didn't look too pleased about. He was hoping you'd drop dead.*

'Does that animal never stop begging?' said Claude grumpily, as Pazzo wagged his tail excitedly at the sight of a piece of ham.

Just as well you didn't see me slip him that big chunk of cheese.

'And that lead,' Claude complained. It was a piece of string, donated by the hotel receptionist. 'We can't walk around Venice with a dog on that. People will think we're a gang of Gypsies.'

Gypsies? Why Gypsies? I'm sure their dogs have very good leads. Leather, probably. And seeing as you're wearing a top-notch Savile Row suit – which Mother probably paid for – is it likely that anyone will think you're a Gypsy, just because I have a dog on a piece of string? But then Julius realized his stepfather's sourness could offer the very chance he was seeking. 'I can go and get a lead,' he offered. 'I've finished my breakfast, so for that matter I can go right now.' *He's weighing fears. Fear of a lunatic son roaming free and fear of being sneered at.*

'If you want to, I suppose.' He took out his wallet and gave Julius twenty lire. 'That should do it.'

Oh good – the fear of sneers won.

Shortly afterwards, Julius walked out into Venice, a free man with his dog. *It's even better in daylight. How strong the sun is down here, warm on my face. The light's different, too. It almost seems a little purple. Perhaps it's the sea all around.* The desk clerk at the hotel had told him he would find newspaper sellers by St Mark's Square and he set out, asking directions as he went. *Pazzo's so wilful, dragging me along. It really does seem like he's trying to tell me something. Or the Predictor?* Julius made an effort to study the dog's behaviour. *You bark at poor people – anybody in old, dirty clothes. No, you don't like them at all. I wonder what that can mean? And children – you can't stand children. But you like anyone in a uniform. You always wag your tail if you see a policeman, or a soldier or one of the fascists. See, you're even doing it at that gondolier. Is he with the Predictor?* It didn't seem very likely.

Now why are you pulling me into this little courtyard,

Pazzo? He felt a slight shudder. *Was one of the Other's agents following me along that lane?* Julius glanced back but saw, with relief, that nobody was coming after him. *Oh, it's that.* He tugged at the string to stop Pazzo tipping over a dustbin. *Nice, smelly rubbish.* But Julius didn't return to the lane. *We'll find another way, just in case.* Now he found himself being dragged onto a bridge over a canal. *Oh, now you want to be friends with this nice little dog. Actually, I think it's a girl dog and it's not friendship you're after. She seems quite keen.* 'That's enough of that, Pazzo.' The other animal's owner, a woman wearing a fur coat, though the day was anything but cold, had been lost in conversation with a man in an old-fashioned hat, and, as she turned round, her eyes opened wide and she hurriedly scooped up her pet. *No need to give me that look – it's not my fault.* Julius frowned, wondering. *Were you trying to warn me about her?* He made a mental note of the woman's face.

St Mark's Square was lightly sprinkled with tourists, feeding corn to the swathes of pigeons or posing for photographs and, just as the desk clerk at the hotel had promised, Julius saw several newspaper kiosks. *That's odd. I don't see any foreign papers here, just Italian ones.* 'Manchester Guardian?' he asked. The salesman gave him an insistent shake of his head. 'No. Qui in Italia non abbiamo giornali stranieri.'

Whatever that means. I'll try another.

He did, and then a third, with growing unease, as both gave what sounded like much the same answer. At a fourth kiosk the salesman spoke a little English. 'No foreign newspapers in Italy,' he said. 'Except this.' Secretively, he took a paper from beneath a pile of others, that was titled L'Osservatore Romano.

'But that's Italian too,' said Julius, confused.

'No, no,' said the salesman. 'Vaticano. Pope's paper.'

Well, it's no use to me, that's for sure. Julius felt faintly sick. *I don't understand. It said everything would be fine.*

He sat on a step at the side of the cathedral, opposite a small stone lion, till two men in fascist uniforms walked up. 'No sitting here.'

'Sorry.'

Pazzo excitedly wagged his tail at the militiamen. *Why didn't you warn me, dog? Unless you tried to and I didn't understand.* An unwelcome thought came to Julius. *Or unless it wasn't the Predictor who sent you but the Other.* He managed to shrug it away. *No, you're not against me, Pazzo. You're good. There's an answer to all of this, there must be. I just have to find it.* And then, to his surprise and relief, he did. *Of course — why on earth didn't I think of it before? It's so obvious. I'll just take it there myself. Sorry, Lou. But then I won't miss your wedding, because there won't be one.* Pazzo was looking up at him. *Don't worry, I won't leave you to Claude – I wouldn't dream of it. And besides, I'll need you. You'll give me signs and help keep me safe.*

Julius found his way to the desk of the tourist information office and explained that he wanted to take a train that day to Manchester. 'Yes, London's fine. I can find my way from there.' *Five-fifty-five? That's perfect, plenty of time. And I can get a ticket at the station, so that's easy, too.* But his smile left him when he asked the lire exchange rate and counted his money. *Damn. Even with the Austrian Schillings, I don't have quite enough. And I'll need food, too, including some for you, Pazzo.* He stood outside the office, wondering. *Harriet and Harold have money. I'm sure they'll help me. They of all people should understand.* But then he saw another difficulty. *Claude has my passport. Damn and damn again. Don't get in a bother. Stay calm. One thing at a time. There'll be an answer to this, too, I'm sure.* Julius tugged at the string to stop Pazzo from barking at a small, startled girl.

He bought lire at a bureau de change, keeping a little sterling for the ticket to Manchester, and it was only when he walked away that he glimpsed Pazzo's leash and remembered the reason he had given for venturing out. *There must be a pet shop somewhere.* Now that he began looking, though, he realized that most shops were closed. *What's going on? Damn, of course. It's Easter Monday. I suppose I'd better ask anyway*. He tried people who looked scruffy, supposing that they were more likely to be Venetians and not tourists, and after trying several, he found himself adopted by a small, sad-faced man who led him to a shuttered shop and then to a nearby bar where the owner of the pet shop was having a coffee. Obligingly, she led him inside through a back door and moments later Julius emerged, much surprised by his success.

And it was only ten lire. That leaves another ten for the journey. A thought came to him. *And after I get there? What then? I'll be alone in Manchester with Pazzo and hardly a penny.* He batted it away. *By then everything will be all right. The Manchester Guardian will be amazed by what I've brought them, they'll print it, all the world will change and I'll be a hero. Everything will be right as rain. Right as right can be. And don't you look smart now, Pazzo?* 'Though you don't seem very happy,' he said aloud. The dog kept twisting his head and trying to pull off the new leather lead with his paw. *It's already almost twelve. Harriet and Harold will probably be at the hotel by now.* Julius hurried down the crowded lane, only to find that the lead, which had been slack, as Pazzo trotted along beside him, was suddenly pulled from his hand. *Where have you gone?* Julius could see no sign of the animal among the striding legs. He hurried ahead and then, finding nothing, retraced his steps, calling out, 'Pazzo! Pazzo!' People gave him curious looks. *It's not my fault that's his name.* He fought down a sense of panic. *Is this the Predictor's doing? Is it angry with me? What can I have done? Unless it's the Other.* Then, just as he was losing heart, he reached the spot where Pazzo had first absconded and found him sitting on his haunches by the side of the lane, panting. Seeing Julius, he jumped up and padded towards him.

There was no sign of the leather lead. *How did you get it off? Just as well I still have the string.* Julius took it from his pocket and Pazzo waited patiently for it to be placed around his neck. *You like this string.* Julius toured nearby lanes but the just-purchased lead was nowhere to be found. *Someone's probably taken it. Unless you threw it into a canal. I wouldn't put it past you, Pazzo. Claude will be furious. But there's no time to go back and get another now. And besides, you'd probably just chuck that away too.*

When he finally reached the hotel, Julius found a note waiting for him, written in his stepfather's neat, leaning script.

Where the hell have you got to? We're all at Il Pescatore, just across the road on the left. Expecting you there very SOON.

It's like he's rabid. The word set off a troubling realization. *Oh hell, I hadn't thought of that. They won't let Pazzo into England because of rabies. Never mind, never mind, there'll be some way. I'll hide you in my pocket or under my jacket. Or in my suitcase, if I get a chance to get it out of the room.* The train of thought brought a happier notion. *That'll solve one problem, and it's actually the most difficult.* 'Can I have my passport?' he asked.

The receptionist checked. 'Mr Reid took them all.'

With all the nonchalance he could muster, Julius asked for the key, not to his and Frank's room, but to Claude and Lilian's. *Good, yes, we're all the same to him.* Into the small lift he went. *Let's hope Claude didn't take them with him to Il Pescatore.* He unlocked the door, walked inside and for a moment he stood, feeling the strangeness of finding himself there. The room had been cleaned, the bedcover was perfectly smoothed down and everything was neat and tidy. Lilian's trunk was on the luggage rack and he saw a novel she was reading on the side table. He could smell her perfume in the air and even the faint musk of old jackets that lingered around Claude. *What if they send out a police alert, some international thing, and I'm stopped on the way?* He shook his head then shook it again. 'I'm not throwing everything away out of fear,' he said, aloud. He began searching the room and in the second place he looked, a drawer in a bedside table, he found the slim leather case where Claude kept his travel papers and, just as he had hoped, all five passports were inside. *Thank you kindly, Stepfather.* Leaving the key at the front desk, he crossed the road to the restaurant. *Now I just have to get Harriet and Harold alone for a moment.* Walking into the restaurant, though, he saw that this wouldn't be easy, as the only empty seat at the table was between Frank and Claude. *That's what comes of being last.*

'Hello, half-brother,' said Harriet, darting Julius a significant glance.

That's to remind me of my promise to smash up Lou's wedding. As if I could forget.

'Hello, half-brother-in-law,' said Harold.

He hasn't changed that much in ten years. He still has that vague smile when he looks at you, like he's thinking of something else.

'And hello stray dog, the famous Pazzo,' said Harriet. 'What a nice piece of string he has.'

Here it comes.

'Where's his new lead?' demanded Claude. 'You had the whole morning. What the hell were you doing?'

'I got one, even though it's Easter Monday, and everywhere was shut, but then Pazzo gave me the slip and chucked it away. I searched everywhere. I think he prefers the string.' *He doesn't believe me.* On another day Julius might have let it pass but today he didn't feel like being thought a liar. From his pocket he took a receipt that the pet shop woman had carefully written out for him and handed it to Claude, who glanced at it distantly. *Not that he cares but everyone knows I'm telling the truth.* Julius tried to catch Harriet's eye but she was playing Slimers with her brother and sister. *What a sight. The young British fascist, the Hitler adorer and the devoted communist, all chirping and hooting over a pack of filthy old playing cards.* Harold was disdainfully filling his pipe. *My half-brother-in-law looks quite left out. Perhaps I'll be able to catch his notice.* But before Julius could try, Harold began helping his parents-in-law with the menu. *Who'd have thought he'd speak good Italian? If he was going to be fluent in something I'd have expected it to be Russian.*

'I wouldn't advise it, Mrs Reid,' he told Lilian, when she expressed interest in the penne with artichoke. 'Not in Venice. Artichoke's very much a Roman ingredient and I'd wait till you get there. I myself will be choosing the spaghetti al nero di seppia – that's spaghetti with black squid ink – as you can't do better here.'

Pasta with squid ink? What d'you think of that, Pazzo?

Maude glanced up from her Slimers. 'You're awfully knowledgeable about good eating for a man of the workers,' she goaded him.

'And why not?' Harold answered, chewing the end of his empty pipe. 'Culture's for everyone, not just the bourgeoisie. After the revolution, everybody will be able to eat in a place like this. And they'll go to the theatre, to concerts and galleries.'

'Everyone except you, Mo Mo,' Harriet said to Maude with a smile, 'as you'll be six feet under. The commissars will deal with you and your Nazis in no time.'

Maude broke into a dreamy smile. 'Once dear Hitler sorts everything out, even scarpering off to Moscow won't save you, Doodle.'

If the revolution does come, I don't see you lasting very long, Harold. Not the owner of Wisbury Hall. He imagined Harriet pointing an accusing finger at him and delivering a stream of denunciations. *Yes, Harriet will probably survive all right, but not Harold.*

The food arrived and Julius was enjoying a final forkful of spaghetti with squid ink – *Harold was right, it's delicious. And you liked it, too, Pazzo. Look at your inky-black muzzle* – when he was surprised to catch the stare of a large man with a handlebar moustache, who was sitting alone a couple of tables away. *Are you watching us, Walrus? Now you've disappeared behind your paper. Probably not.* But the suspicion lingered. *Who could have sent you? Nazis? They might have, if they got poor Joachim to tell them about giving me his notes.*

Or fascists? Lou's fiancé? I can't think he'd know about Harriet's scheme or Joachim's notes, but he might? Julius felt a moment of vague, oppressive unease. *Or the Other.* He glanced towards the man alone at his table. *Are you looking at us again, Walrus?* It was hard to tell, as his eyes were exactly aligned with the top of the paper.

Julius was just wondering how he might get Harriet's attention – *cup my mouth with my hands and mime to her that I need to talk?* – but then found that there was no need after all, as she and Harold got up from their seats and began edging their way round the table towards Julius. 'Sorry, my dearies,' she said, 'but we have to beetle.'

'You haven't had coffee,' said Claude.

'Things to do,' Harold insisted. 'Change money, book trains, that sort of nonsense.'

'Dearest Ma and Pa, I'm going to steal away the half-brother for a short walk, if that's all right,' Harriet told them, 'as I haven't seen him for years and Harold hasn't since he was a spotty little schoolboy.'

Claude gave a courteous nod. 'As you like.' He glanced at Julius. 'But come straight back this time, will you?'

'Of course, don't worry.' *That was easy. Thank you, Predictor.* Julius followed them out, Pazzo trotting at his feet. *No time to waste, no time for chit-chat.* 'I need you to do me a favour,' he said. 'It's awfully important.'

'Me first,' said Harriet firmly, as they walked. 'I hope you haven't forgotten our little scheme?'

'Of course not,' said Julius. 'I doubt I'll be back from Manchester in time for the wedding but it won't matter now as the whole thing will be called off anyway.'

'What on earth are you talking about?' Harriet looked baffled. 'Manchester?'

'That's the favour I need to ask you,' Julius told her. 'I need to leave today and I don't have quite enough money for the train.' He took Joachim's pages from his pocket and hurriedly explained to them about the visit to Dachau and Joachim shoving against him, how he had found the pages in his pocket and realized that they could bring down the Nazis, and Mussolini, too, and finally his vain search for the Manchester Guardian's address.

Harriet gave him a doubtful look and peered at the pages. 'I wish I knew German. Harold?'

'Not a word.'

'And we can't very well show it to Maude.' She frowned. 'I can't believe this will be enough to topple Hitler, let alone Mussolini, though that's not to say it may not be useful.'

'It must be important,' Julius insisted, 'or he wouldn't have taken such a risk passing it to me.'

'Whatever it is, I wouldn't waste your time sending it to

the Manchester Guardian,' said Harold loftily. 'It's an awful rag, and no better than the Tory ones. A crowd of bourgeois reactionaries, leftist romantics and utopian socialists. If you want to send it to a paper, the only one to consider is the Daily Worker. They'll translate it in a jiffy. And I can give you their address right now.'

'Or we could send it straight to someone in the party,' said Harriet, giving Harold a look. 'I'm sure they'd be interested.'

That would be much easier. But Julius knew he couldn't do any such thing. He pointed to the last lines. 'This is what Joachim wanted and I'm not letting him down. He put his trust in me.' *And that's what the Predictor expects.* A shape to his left caught his eye. *That man in the alpine hat with his back to us, looking into the window of the umbrella shop?*

'Even if you do send it to the Manchester Guardian,' said Harriet, 'there's no need to go haring all the way back to England. Harold and I can make a couple of phone calls from the hotel and find out the address.'

Julius felt a weight lift from him. *Then I won't have to worry about getting Pazzo across the Channel to England. Or where'll he'll shit on the train.*

'If you trust the Italian post, that is,' said Harold, 'which I can't say I do. When will you be in Rome?'

Julius tried to think. 'Tomorrow we go to Cousin Ivor in Tuscany but that's just one night. So we should be there the following evening.'

'Then it couldn't be simpler,' said Harold. 'When you get there, take yourself off to the Foreign Press Club, or the Foreign Correspondent's Club, or whatever it is they call themselves. I went there once and it's over by the Trevi Fountain. Then ask who's with the Manchester Guardian. Whoever it is, he'll know someone who can translate it, and if it's as important as you think it is, then he can wire it straight to Manchester and Bob's your uncle. If you get it in early, it'll be in print the next morning.'

Julius smiled, amazed. *Why didn't I think of that? Then I don't know anything about newspapers.* He made an effort to memorize what he had been told. *Foreign Press Club. Somewhere by the Trevi Fountain.*

Harriet had seen his concentration. 'We'll be there by then, too, so we can give you a hand.'

Better and better. Then, though, Julius felt his smile fading away. Reflected in the window of the umbrella shop, he was just able to make out the faint curve of a moustache. *It is you, Walrus.* 'That man over there,' he said in a low voice, nodding his head to point. 'I saw him in the restaurant. I'm sure he's following me.'

Harold looked uneasy. 'I didn't see him.'

'And I certainly didn't,' agreed Harriet.

'Of course you didn't. You both had your backs to him,' said Julius impatiently. *They're looking at me oddly. Am I speaking too fast?* 'And you were playing Slimers, Harriet, while Harold was busy showing off his Italian.'

'Are you sure you're all right, Ju?' she asked. 'You're not . . .'

Why can nobody say it?

But then she did. '. . . you're not going a bit potty again, are you?'

Julius felt stung. *Why would she think that?* 'I'm fine, absolutely fine,' Julius insisted. *Good as can be. Good as gold.* 'Never been better. Look, I'd probably best be off, as I said I wouldn't be gone long.'

'If we don't see you here then we'll see you in Rome, eh?' said Harold a little warily.

'And remember, no bottling out,' added Harriet with a warning glance.

Didn't she listen to what I just told her? I won't have to wreck the wedding, as everything's about to change. Everything's going to be fine. But as he began walking back towards the hotel, Julius' sense of certainty began to ebb. *Perhaps I should have stuck with them rather than going off alone?* He felt an urge to glance round. *Is Walrus following me, Pazzo?* The dog trotted quietly along by his feet, not tugging at his string, and giving no signs. *If I look, then he'll know I know, which won't be good. He'll barge into me, I bet, then I'll reach into my pocket and find it's gone.* That moment, of discovering in one instant that everything was lost, the sense of shock and panic, came to him with disturbing clarity, almost as if it had actually happened. He buttoned up his jacket but it didn't feel tight enough. *Or somebody else will do it. Another agent.* Imaginings came to him. A stiletto blade, so slim and sharp that he'd hardly feel it stab. *Is this the way we came? These lanes all look the same. I should have paid more attention before, but we were so busy talking. Should I stay in this alleyway, where it's crowded and it'll be harder to see him? Or take that one, which is empty so I'll hear him behind me. No, definitely not. There'd be no witnesses, nobody to make him think twice.*

Out of nowhere, a memory came to him. *Where was that? I was walking down a crowded street just like this, worried for my life. Though that time I was the pursuer not the pursued.* It came back to him. *In Twickenham, when I was following the white slavers who were after Linda. The ones who I saw watching her at the film studio.* For just a moment the oddest thought came to Julius. *Is this the same?* Into his mind's eye came Dr Morrison's face, that seemed far too open, pretending it had no secrets, like a mother to a child. *If you have any strange thoughts . . .* Julius felt an unknowingness spread

through him, like a disease. Even his steps felt wrong –
awkward and tentative. *That slippiness. Anything but that.*
And then, when he needed it most, a notion came to help
him. *Of course, that's why he was sent.* He picked up Pazzo
and held him close to his face. 'Save me, Predictor, please,'
he murmured. 'Make everything clear and right. Tell me
what to do.' A part of him half expected Pazzo to open his
mouth and speak, but instead he licked Julius' cheek, as
words appeared from nowhere in Julius' head. *Clench your
right hand three times.*

Putting Pazzo back on the ground, Julius did as he'd
heard and clenched his right hand three times into a fist.
Was that too fast, so it seemed like one clench? For certainty,
he clenched three times more slowly. He walked below a
statue of a man in a helmet sitting on a plump-looking horse.
Do I dare look now? He turned and glanced back, then peered
round the other side of the horse's legs, and, to his amazement, his joy and relief, there was no sign of Walrus. *Unless
there's someone else. Should I check?* In an instant he had gone
from a state of panic to one of certainty, even a kind of
whimsical confidence. Clenching his fist three times more,
he set off down a narrow, deserted alleyway. Hearing his
footsteps echo and feeling the cool damp of the lane all
around him, he glanced back, glanced back again and
laughed. *Nobody. Thank you, Predictor.* 'And thank you,

Pazzo.' *The Foreign Press Club near the Trevi Fountain. The Foreign Press Club near the Trevi Fountain. Actually, this is better, better even than posting it from Austria, which might've taken ages. Everything's going to be all right now, everything's going to be fine.*

Six

Julius clenched his hand whenever it wouldn't attract notice and, as he had hoped, he saw no sign of Walrus that afternoon, when he walked round the art gallery with his family, where Lilian cooed over the many Madonnas and Bambinos. Nor did he see him at dinner that evening, where Harriet and Harold once again failed to appear, this time announcing their absence with a brief telephone call – *they knew, that's why they said see you in Rome* – nor afterwards in St Mark's Square, where Julius and his family stood in the cool, sea-smelling air, listening to an orchestral concert. *It definitely scares him off. Clever Predictor, clever Pazzo.* Nor did he see Walrus the next morning, when the family made their way back to the car park. Julius watched from the gondola as the Austin drew slowly nearer, the Innsbruck lamp making its profile resemble an open mouth with a single lower tooth. *Goodbye, beautiful Venice. I liked you even if you gave me some scares.*

The first hour's driving was easy, along the straight roads of the Po Valley plain. As they went, Julius felt a joy rise within him, as if his stomach were full of bubbles. *South, south, south. Now everything will be perfectly fine.* But to be on the safe side, he continued to clench his hand, which was now conveniently hidden beneath Pazzo. *You don't seem to mind. Then you wouldn't, seeing as you were the one who told me to do it.* When he was able, he turned round in his seat, ostensibly to make himself more comfortable, but really to glance through the small rear window. For a time he was concerned by a black car that appeared and disappeared from sight some distance behind them, but then it vanished altogether. *It's working.* Sure enough, when they next stopped, at a café where Lilian needed to use the lavatory – she emerged looking pale and shaken – there was no other car to be seen on the road. *Predictor, have we lost them?* Though Julius heard no reply, he wasn't troubled. *It's not answering because it doesn't need to. Of course we've lost them.*

'Why d'you keep looking back like that?' asked Frank when they set out once more. 'D'you think someone's coming after you?'

Another time Julius might have shrunk away at the question but not today. *I'm not going to be pestered by you, you goading little squirt.* 'Why are you so scared of wasps?' he demanded back. 'Why did you pee your pants that time when one landed on your head? Why can't you eat cheese? Why did all your sisters call you crybaby?'

Frank looked shocked. 'But that's all just a lot of nonsense.'

'What's going on back there?' asked Claude, turning round in his seat and causing Lilian to cover her eyes.

'He's saying a lot of silly nonsense.'

'Well, don't,' said Claude.

But Frank will think twice before he bothers me again.

After a quick stop to eat their packed lunches, which had been provided by the Venice hotel, they began to climb along winding roads into the Apennines, and Claude told them about his cousin Ivor. 'You and he will get on like a house on fire, Frank,' he said, twisting round and giving him a wink. 'He's a real adventurer, in the very best English way. He was just too young for the war, poor chap, but he's lived a quite extraordinary life. And he's a flyer, like you want to be.'

Another dictator of the future? Claude's delighted to have found a relative he can boast about, for once. Mother's are so much more prestigious.

Cousin Ivor, so Claude told them, had trained as a pilot with the air force after leaving school, and then had worked in Canada, ferrying passengers from town to town, 'but of course that was far too tame for Ivor'. Next he had worked in Arabia, 'in some sheikh's air force. Actually, from what Ivor said, he was the whole air force, pretty much.' Claude roared with laughter at the very thought. For a time Ivor had joined with another pilot to run a cattle ranch in Australia, 'till he realized the other chap was a cheat and a bounder, so Ivor gave him a punch on the nose and bade him sayonara. Then he was a bodyguard for a businessman in Istanbul, dodgy chap but he paid well, Ivor said. And now he's here in Tuscany, a gentleman farmer, making his own wine and olive oil and that sort of thing.' Claude laughed again. 'Ivor making wine – the very idea! I'm sure it's absolute gut-rot.'

Little Frank's eyes are glistening. A new hero for you to worship.

'He does sound most interesting,' said Lilian distantly.

She always has to show her family's better. But this time I rather agree. Ivor sounds awful.

By late afternoon they had reached a small town that clung to a hillside overlooking a wide, flat valley, and was close to where Ivor lived, and thereafter they followed directions that he had sent to them by post. 'He has the most awful handwriting,' Lilian complained. 'I can hardly make out a word.'

It wasn't long before Claude was asking directions in his curious French. 'The natives aren't especially friendly,' he observed, after a woman who'd been sweeping the steps of her house answered not with words but with a scowl and a jab of her finger pointing the way.

Or they don't much like Cousin Ivor.

'And here we are at last,' said Claude, a little too cheerfully, as they stopped in front of a small, run-down-looking stone house.

You were expecting something better. So much for your heroic dictator of the future.

Out they climbed and Claude knocked, calling out, 'Ivor, old chap, we're here,' only to be met with silence. He knocked again. 'That's odd,' he said as they stood waiting outside the closed door. 'When I rang him from Venice yesterday, he said he'd be here.'

'Unless we've come to the wrong place,' said Maude languidly.

'Could be,' Claude agreed.

You hope.

But then when they walked round the house, Claude glanced through a window and gave a shake of his head. 'No, this is Ivor's place all right. I know that painting on the wall. It used to be in his parents' place in Leatherhead. I think it's his grandfather.'

Julius peered in and saw a portrait of a gloomy-looking man with a long beard.

'That's queer,' said Frank. 'I'm almost sure I saw a face, up at that window. It looked like a woman. But there's nobody now.'

They all stepped back from the house and began calling out, 'Hello,' 'Cousin Ivor,' 'We're here,' but, as before, they were met with silence.

'It was probably just some shadow,' said Claude doubtfully. 'I'm sure he'll turn up in no time.'

'But he could be hours,' said Lilian. 'And I have to say I'm getting awfully hungry. I suggest we go back to that town and get some dinner. We can always ring him from there to see if he's come back.'

I won't be too bothered if he never turns up. Then we can get to Rome sooner. A cheering thought came to Julius. *What if this isn't chance and it's all the Predictor's doing, to give me a hand?* 'I'm quite hungry, too,' he agreed.

'And me,' said Maude.

'Very well, then, if you're all so starved,' said Claude, a little sourly, and they made their way back to the car.

When all this is over, if Louisa's lonely, or just sad, as she probably will be, having given her fascist the boot, we could go and live somewhere together, just us two. On a little island perhaps.

They reached the town and drove through winding streets that at times seemed barely wider than the Austin, and which, rather to Julius' surprise, Claude managed to negotiate with nothing worse than the slight scraping of a wing mirror. They parked in a small square.

'There's a little hotel,' Lilian pointed out as they walked through the town. 'We can always stay there.'

'I'm sure we won't need to, Pet,' said Claude keenly.

In Scotland perhaps? There are lots of islands there. It wouldn't be easy for us to earn a living, of course. And Lou probably wouldn't want to be stuck with her brother in the middle of nowhere, as she'll want to be busy, going out, so she can find someone new. For that matter, she may want to stick in Rome, as she has a job there. But she might like it, mightn't she?

They found a restaurant that was crowded with local people, and where Claude urged everyone to order pasta, as it would be faster. He ate his own in moments and then hurried off in search of a telephone. *I'm sure you won't have any luck.* But Julius was wrong and Claude returned in triumph.

'Ivor was full of apologies. He had to help a neighbour with something and got held up. We must have just missed him. He can't wait to see us, and his housekeeper has more dinner ready for us if we're still hungry. A shame we didn't wait a little longer.'

'We weren't to know,' said Lilian simply.

A croft can't cost much to rent. And there must be some

kind of work to do. Lou could knit sweaters and I could fish. I've never caught anything bigger than sticklebacks but I could ask a local fisherman to teach me. There must be plenty of them in places like that. And it can't be so very hard. You go out in a boat with a net and . . .

Julius' thoughts were interrupted by the clattering of shutters being lowered at a nearby shop. *It's almost eight. They stay open so late here.* Just ahead were two women and a man, walking slowly and blocking the narrow road, causing Claude to make impatient coughs. *I bet ten guineas they're a mother and daughter, even though I can only see them from behind. They're the same height and the one on the left is thin with an hourglass figure, while the one on the right is heavier and more filled out. They even have the same birdlike sort of walk. And the man, struggling with all those shopping bags – they look like food – will be their servant. No, he's wearing a cap, so he's the chauffeur. I imagine they'll be from one of the richer families in this little town. There can't be many people here who have a car and driver.*

Reaching the Austin, they took their seats and Claude turned on the ignition, saying, 'I remember the most hilarious story about Cousin Ivor. Years ago, when we were both . . .' He got no further because there was then a loud crunching sound and Julius felt himself pressed against his seat, his head jerked backwards.

Are you all right, Pazzo? But he seemed quite untroubled, jumping up to lick Julius' face. *Thank goodness.*

'Not again?' said Lilian. 'Really, Claude, I can't believe this.'

Nor can I. But when they all climbed out of the car, Julius saw that, this time, his mother was being a little unfair. The rear of the Austin was crumpled into the back of another car that was newer and sleeker than theirs. From the positions of the two vehicles in the very centre of the small piazza, it was clear what had happened. They had reversed into one another, so both drivers were equally at fault.

We'd better not get stuck here like we did in Innsbruck. Julius was startled by a piercing cry that broke the quiet and he saw three figures emerging from the other car. *It's them. Definitely mother and daughter.* It was the daughter who had called out and her shriek now became a torrent of furious words. *That doesn't sound good.* A suspicion came to him like a faint whiff of sulphur. *Was this an accident?*

Claude's attempts to reply, 'Ce n'est pas entièrement de ma faute, Mesdames, pas entièrement de ma faute,' were drowned out by the daughter's cries.

Julius glanced at the Austin. *Actually, it's not too bad.* Lilian's trunk, which had struck the back of the other car, had split, with garments emerging through the crack, and it hung down precariously from the rack it perched on,

196

which was badly bent. Looking more closely, Julius saw that the rear of the car had been dented inwards by the force of the collision. *And the number plate's come off. But it should still drive, even if it looks awful. Who's she calling out to?* The daughter was shouting and, despite his lack of Italian, Julius was able to make out one of her words – 'polizia'. In answer, several small boys, who had wandered over to see the excitement, now scampered away. *I don't like the look of that.* Julius pondered in the darkness. *I didn't see their car here when we first arrived. I bet they parked in that place deliberately so they'd be ready for us to reverse. And that'll be why they were walking in front of us when we left the restaurant. They'd been waiting for us to finish our meals.* He frowned. *Now what's she up to?*

The daughter said something to the chauffeur who climbed back into the car, started up the motor and began driving forwards into the parking place they had just vacated. The rear bumpers of the two cars were so enmeshed that Lilian's car was dragged backwards with his. *Now it looks like it was all our fault. Predictor, help.*

Claude, briefly speechless, guffawed into life. 'But this is outrageous. A dirty, stinking trick.'

Even Lilian was won round. 'It's dreadful,' she agreed.

'That would never happen in Germany,' said Maude primly. 'In Germany when there's any accident, everyone knows that they're not allowed to move anything, not even an inch.'

Julius' sense of foreboding grew. *Who's behind this, that's the question. Hitler? Lou's Freddy? The Other?*

'Vous êtes tricheuses, mesdames,' Claude railed at the mother and daughter, 'sales, méchantes tricheuses,' but then a half-smile passed across his face and he murmured, 'Quick, let's get into the car.'

A good idea for once.

They hurried into their seats, Pazzo jumping onto Julius' lap, but escape proved hard. The women's chauffeur, still in the driving seat, applied his brakes so his car could not be dragged, while the two vehicles were so locked together that, though Claude pressed hard on the accelerator, filling the piazza with noise and fumes, he couldn't break free. Julius clenched his right hand three times, six times, nine times, twelve. *Why isn't it working? Perhaps I should try both hands?* He did so but with no more success. *What if it cancelled out the ones I did before?* He began trying again only with his right hand but then he heard a furious thumping sound and, looking up, he saw the faces of the mother and daughter inches from the windscreen, as they hammered their hands on the glass, shouting, 'Fermi, fermi!'

'Just go anyway,' Frank urged his father. 'It's their lookout. They shouldn't be there.'

Yes, just go.

But Claude switched off the engine. 'I have no wish to be arrested for murder, however much they deserve it.' The two women stopped their thumping and began waving in the direction the boys had run. Following their glances, Julius saw that a small group of uniformed figures was advancing across the square towards them, led by a stout, scowling man in a large cap. The small boys ran beside him, grinning at the drama they had helped bring about. Julius felt a chill pass through him. *Is that Walrus? No, he just has the same kind of moustache.* He climbed out of the car, his legs feeling strangely stiff.

The police had brought an English-speaker – *all these little towns seem to have one. Is that chance?* – through whom Claude vented his disgust. 'These two women are liars and cheats of the worst kind. Don't believe a single word they say.'

As if the police will take any notice? This will all have been planned out hours ago, probably, even days. Something puzzled Julius. *But how did they know we'd be here? Nobody followed our car from Venice – I saw that as we drove.* Then he understood. *They didn't need to. They'll have tapped the telephone line when Claude rang Cousin Ivor yesterday.* A more disturbing thought came to him. *I bet that's why Cousin Ivor wasn't there. They've taken him. Whoever Claude rang just now will have been an impersonator.* He patted his hand against his jacket to feel Joachim's pages in his pocket, but felt little comfort, and his unease soon seemed fully justified. The chief policeman listened to the mother, her daughter and their driver with sympathetic smiles, while towards Claude he was disdainfully aloof. Though he questioned a couple of witnesses, the English-speaker was cagey as to their answers, while even Frank's triumphant discovery of a broken rear lamp at the spot where the collision had occurred made no impression.

'The commander of the police says it is not important as it rolled there from the incident,' the English-speaker explained. Then, in the midst of the questioning, three men in overalls appeared.

Mechanics. What are they doing here? Are they going to do something to our car so we can't get away? Instead, using crowbars, they separated the two vehicles. *Now the luggage rack is worse and the dent in the back looks terrible.* The mechanics drove Lilian's car a few yards free and then turned all their attention towards the damage done to the other vehicle. After a brief consultation among the three, one of them murmured a few words to the chief policeman.

'The commander of the police says you are very fortunate,' the English-speaker translated. 'There will be no crime charges if you pay three hundred and two lire for the damage you did to the ladies' car.'

Julius tried to hold in his hope. *It's a chance to get away. Unless it's a trick. But perhaps my clenching worked after all? Just say yes, Claude, please.*

'I absolutely refuse,' Claude replied. 'As the freeborn citizen of a land where, I'm happy to say, justice reigns, I will not pay these people a penny, not in a thousand . . .'

The translator interrupted with a simplified version of his answer. 'Dice no.' At a nod from the chief policeman, Claude found his wrists handcuffed, the fallen number plate was plucked from the ground and Lilian was alarmed into handing over Claude's passport. Claude had been arrested, the translator explained, for dangerous driving and attempting to flee from an accident.

'But this is disgraceful,' Claude bellowed. 'I demand to speak to the British Ambassador.'

It was all a bluff – they knew he'd say no. But I don't understand. The Predictor promised . . . Julius realized his mistake. *No, it didn't promise anything. It said everything would be all right if I make it happen. Does that mean I've failed in some way? But how?*

As Claude was led from the square, the other members of the family began following, only for Lilian to stop. 'We can't leave our things here. They could be stolen.'

'We could put your trunk inside the car,' suggested Frank.

'But that won't help.'

It was true, as the Austin's doors had no locks.

Julius glanced across the little square to a long, beckoning street. *Should I just go while I have the chance? Find a railway station, if there is one, and take a train straight to Rome? I have the money that I changed in Venice. But they're sure to have somebody watching the station. I could run off into the countryside? Lie down under an olive tree.* For a moment the peacefulness of the prospect seemed appealing. *But that'll be just what they want. To catch me alone in the middle of nowhere without witnesses? Make me disappear, like people do. In Russia and Germany. From the white slavers. A vanished lunatic – nobody'd think there's anything odd in that.*

'Give me a hand, will you?' said Frank crossly.

Julius helped him loosen the belts around Lilian's trunk and they heaved it off the broken rack. *What's she got in here? It weighs half a ton.* Lilian and Maude carried two suitcases each while Julius and Frank struggled with Lilian's trunk, which made creaking sounds with each step they took, and they followed Claude's shouts of, 'I demand to speak to the British Ambassador.' They passed a bar, from which customers spilled out onto the street to watch the spectacle of foreigners being led away in handcuffs, shouting and carrying their own luggage. *The Other has got the whole town against us.*

They soon reached the police station, from within which Julius heard his stepfather's voice and then a clang. *They've put him in the cells.* As they approached the entrance, the English-speaker emerged, giving them a little wave goodbye. *Why's he leaving? I can guess. No witnesses.* Julius felt himself shiver. *Predictor, if I go in there, will they take Joachim's notes? Will I ever come out alive?* There was no answer. *For goodness' sake, why won't you help me, now when I really need help?* At the police station door, Julius stopped and lowered his end of the trunk to the ground.

'What on earth are you doing?' demanded Frank.

'Julius,' said his mother. 'This really isn't the time.'

But being alone out here could be even riskier than being in there. So he changed his mind and picked up the trunk, shuffled inside and took his place with the others on a long bench. *Stay calm, stay calm.* He made himself look around the room. *Who's that in the portrait? It must be the Italian king. He looks very small on the horse. But his picture's much bigger than Mussolini's. They like the king in here.* The police chief had retreated to his office, but the door was open and Julius could see him, sitting at his desk, leafing through papers. *That's odd. He looks a little nervous, even scared. But*

who of? Walrus? Or his bosses? Whoever they are? The Other?
Julius felt the string slip out of his hand and watched,
dismayed, as Pazzo padded away, the leash trailing behind
him, and sat on the shoe of one of the policemen, who
glanced down and absent-mindedly stroked his head. *Are
you trying to tell me something? But what?*

The police station was quiet and though the cells were
out of view, Julius could hear his stepfather clearly enough.
You're trying a new tack.

'Je suis un fasciste,' Claude called out. 'Fasciste anglais.
Je connais très bien Oswald Mosley. Fascisti, fascisti. I can
show you my badge, damn it.'

His shouts inspired his family, and Frank held up his
BUF junior pin and his swastika badge, too, for good
measure. Maude waved all three of her swastikas, declaring,
'I'll have you know that I know lots of very important people
in Germany. Now let him go this moment, you awful people.'
Lilian, for lack of anything else, brandished her reading
glasses case.

As if that'll work.

But, to Julius' surprise, he saw the police chief emerge
from his office and call out, towards nobody in particular, 'Trecento due lire,' and then, in unexpected English,
'Three hundred two lire.' Next he walked round to the
cells, repeating, 'Three hundred two lire,' adding, 'One

telefono.' Julius heard a key turn in a lock and, as he was ushered into the chief's office, Claude shot the others a wink.

'Well done, Pa,' said Frank, grinning. 'He's got them on the run.'

Was that thanks to the Predictor? Julius tried to restrain his hopes as he listened to the faint, flat sound of his stepfather's voice on the telephone. Pazzo licked the hand of the policeman whose shoe he was sitting on. *You're telling me something. Of course – now I understand why you like people in uniforms. You're giving me a sign to tell me who's with the Other? How very ingenious. By pretending you like them, you make sure they don't realize what you're doing.*

Claude had finally emerged but Julius saw that his look of triumph had now vanished. 'Looks like we have to pay up,' he said glumly to Lilian.

Frank was appalled. 'But that's giving in. What did the ambassador say?'

Pay, just pay. As long as we can get out of here.

'I didn't talk to him,' said Claude. 'I rang Cousin Ivor. I knew I wouldn't get through to the embassy at this time of night, while Ivor can ring anyone and get help.'

Lilian rolled her eyes.

If it was Ivor.

'And it turned out he knew all about it,' said Claude,

'and it's damned complicated. It seems the car we had the prang with wasn't just any old car. Ivor knew it right away and he said it's the official car of the local bigwig round here. Something like their mayor.'

Lilian took in a sharp breath. 'So those were his wife and daughter.'

'Actually no, that's something else that's complicated,' said Claude. 'When I described them to Ivor he said they're the bigwig's mistress and her mother.'

Maude scoffed. 'His mistress and her mother using his official car to go shopping? That would never happen in Germany.'

Claude lowered his voice. 'But that's not the end of it. Ivor said the mistress's mother is also a cousin of this police chief chappie. Ivor thinks that the bigwig's away in Perugia right now, while of course the police chief will do his damnedest to pretend they weren't doing anything wrong. He said if we don't pay up, we could be stuck here for days.'

Lies and more lies. Probably. But who cares so long as we can go?

'I'm not missing my daughter's wedding,' said Lilian firmly, and though Maude and Frank objected that it was giving in to an outrageous injustice, she took her traveller's cheques from her handbag, signed a number of them, then counted out the difference with banknotes and called out to the police chief. 'Three hundred and two lire,' she declared, handing it over. In exchange she was given a written receipt and Claude was handed his passport and the car number plate.

Hurrah!

'I can't say I'm at all happy about this,' said Claude, as they walked back through the town, struggling with the luggage. 'But I suppose at least we're free to go.'

Thank heavens! But then, as they reached the small square where they had had the accident, Julius' hopes fell away.

'What the hell's this?' growled Claude. The mother and daughter's car had gone, but theirs remained, marooned in the middle of the piazza, and beside it stood two uniformed figures, together with the English-speaker.

Julius glumly scanned their faces. *No, Walrus isn't here, either. Yes, I see you wagging your tail, Pazzo – but I guessed anyway.*

The English-speaker gave them a friendly wave. 'Good evening again. Now you must go with these fellows to their office.'

'But we've just been, damn it,' said Claude. 'And we've paid for the damage to the other car, which the police had no right to ask for.' He showed them the receipt he had just been given, which they examined with interest.

'No, no,' said the English-speaker in a soothing voice.

'That was policemen. These are MVSN, which means voluntary military of the national security.' He gave a quick smile. 'Fascist ones.'

'There's no use arguing,' said Lilian wearily. 'Let's just do as they ask.'

She's probably right. With a sinking heart, Julius followed the others. *The fascists are pretending to be friendly, helping us with the luggage, but I'm not fooled for a moment.* They passed through a doorway, above which were painted an eagle and a she-wolf suckling Romulus and Remus. The office they entered was shabbier than the police station, its walls covered with fascist banners and pictures of heroic soldiers in battle, while in pride of place was a large, framed portrait of Mussolini. *No sign of the king here. Oh, there he is – a rather small portrait in the corner.* From behind a closed door, Julius heard the muffled sound of a voice shouting questions and another offering quiet, begging answers. *That's where we'll be taken next, I bet. I'll be searched, they'll pretend to be surprised when they find Joachim's document, I'll be arrested. And then . . .* He tried and failed to halt his imagination. *A cell? A beating? The monkey suit? Back to Dachau?*

A militiaman knocked lightly on the door and, as it opened, Julius glimpsed a stout, moustachioed man sitting on a chair with militiamen standing all around him. One of the three officials, whose cap was easily the largest, stepped out of the room towards Julius' family. *The king of whoever these are.* Pazzo wagged his tail. *Yes, I already know.*

The commandant, as the English-speaker explained him to be, ushered the family to sit at a desk, where Claude and Lilian were each presented with a pen and a sheaf of lined paper. 'He asks please to write all about the incident in the piazza,' the English-speaker explained. 'How it happened, the damage, but most of all you must describe the car, the driver and the women.'

'But we've paid,' said Claude, exasperated.

'When you have finished you may go,' the English-speaker continued, oblivious. 'And he says, especially please don't forget to write about their shopping. Say how many bags there were, how big, and anything that you saw inside.' Having assigned them their task, the commandant turned and began talking to one of the militiamen.

Lilian looked baffled. 'Their shopping?'

It does seem strange. Another lie to confuse us? Julius was startled by a cry. The commandant had opened the door to go back into the other room, and Julius glimpsed two of the militiamen holding the moustachioed man on his chair while a third was pushing a funnel into his mouth. Just as the door was closing, Julius saw one of them raising what looked like a bottle of oil. *What are they doing to him?*

'I've got it,' said Frank, delighted with his own insight. 'This lot are trying to get the police into trouble.'

'You know, I think you could be right, Frank,' agreed Claude, nodding. 'Get rid of the rotten apples.'

'If they're not all rotten,' said Maude primly.

'But why?' said Claude. 'I'd rather like to know that, before we get into further trouble.' He pulled out his wallet and turned to the English-speaker, lowering his voice. 'Two lire if you tell us what all this is really about.'

As if he will.

But, to Julius' surprise, the English-speaker glanced briefly about him and then took the purple banknote. 'The truth is, the commander of the volunteer military for national security – the fascisti – is not friends with the podestà – the mayor.'

'Because this podestà chap is a wrong'un?' said Claude, with a sly look.

'Actually, no. You see, many years ago the grandfather of commander Leopoldi said that the podestà's grandfather cheated him of twenty-five olive trees.'

Claude's face lost its keenness. 'I see.'

'And though the case went to the court in Perugia, and for a time it seemed like . . .'

'Is this all going to take a long time?' Lilian interrupted. The English-speaker shrugged. 'Not so long. First you must write about the incident, at least two or three pages so it is correct, with all your full names and date of birth and passport number. Then I must translate everything into Italian, and of course the Italian one must then be controlled and signed by you and by me and by the commandant, and the correct stamps must be put on.'

'How long?'

'An hour,' said the English-speaker brightly. 'Perhaps two or three.'

And by then it'll be so late that nobody will be around to see what happens to us.

'I've got an idea,' said Maude. 'Why don't we ring Lou? Isn't her Freddy some kind of high-up?'

He's the very last one we should ring. 'But we can't,' said Julius suddenly. 'It's late now and she'll be asleep.'

Nobody took any notice. Claude found Louisa's number in his notebook and had the English-speaker ask if he could make a telephone call, claiming he needed to check some details for his statement. Moments later Julius heard the faint sound of Louisa's voice crackling excitedly from the speaker. Claude, fending off her curiosity about their journey, explained the situation as briefly as he could. 'Don't worry, I'll ring Freddy now,' Julius heard Louisa's squeaky voice tell him.

It'll just make things even worse. But to Julius' surprise, soon afterwards the telephone rang. Picking up the receiver, the militiaman who answered looked at first puzzled, then startled and he strode across to the other room, opening the door. *Now the poor man on the chair almost looks like he's crying.* He saw a stain. *Ugh, that's why.*

Hurrying over, the commandant took the telephone and stood stiffly, as if on parade. With a momentary scowl at Claude and the rest of them, he murmured something to the English-speaker.

'He says you may go now,' he translated. 'He says he is sorry for taking your time.'

'I knew Freddy was a bigwig,' murmured Maude proudly as, having said their goodbyes to the translator, they walked outside. A squad of four militiamen accompanied them, carrying all their luggage.

I don't understand at all. But it's good news, I suppose. It must be. Then, though, Julius felt a kind of despairing laugh within him. *I knew it.*

'Not again,' groaned Claude, as he saw that standing beside the Austin were two policemen.

'Didn't the translator say that the police and the fascists all loathe each other?' said Frank excitedly. 'Perhaps there'll be a fight.'

But the four militiamen put the luggage down by the car, greeted the others in an easy way, and then began talking. Clearly, they all knew one another well.

'What's going on?' Claude demanded. 'Que se passe-t-il?'

Reluctantly breaking off from the conversation, one of the police pointed across the piazza, where his superior, the police chief, was panting his way towards them.

'Ecco,' he said, handing Claude an envelope. 'Scusi per l'errore. Mistake. So sorry. And small present for the mistake.'

Tearing it open, Claude found Lilian's traveller's cheques and small sheaf of banknotes. 'Freddy must've rung them, too.'

I still don't understand. But it's definitely good news.

'Three hundred and fifty lire,' said Claude as he sat in the driving seat of the Austin, counting the notes. 'So we're up forty-eight lire. That's two pounds ten, near enough.'

'Not that it'll be anything like enough to cover the new damage to the car,' said Lilian coolly. It was if the Fates had heard and, as they drove off, a loud clattering sound rang out from the rear of the car. But it kept going.

Later that same night Julius lay awake, Pazzo at his side, listening, above the sound of Frank's breathing from the other bed, to whispers from the room next door, which sounded like a brutal, hissed argument. *That'll be Ivor and the woman he says is his housekeeper.* 'What d'you think, Pazzo?' he murmured. *Has Lou's fascist got some other, worse plans for me? Did the Other make a mistake? Did the Predictor save us? Or was there something else that I didn't see? Are the Nazis against the fascists?* Julius smiled in the darkness. *As if I even care. All that matters is that we got away.* 'And tomorrow we'll be in Rome,' he said aloud. 'Probably. With luck. Please, please, I beg you, Predictor, I beg you, please, please.' As Julius murmured the words like a chant, Pazzo stirred and licked his cheek.

Seven

There was a rap at the door and Cousin Ivor's pinched voice called out, 'Breakfast in ten minutes.' Julius breathed in an aroma of wood smoke and, opening his eyes, found there was just enough dawn light coming through the slats of the shutters to reveal a dark smudge on the wall above him. *A stain? No, something with lots of legs.* The air was cool and, as he pulled them on, his clothes were chilly against his skin. He felt strangely exhilarated. *Today nothing can stop me. I'll be like one of those daredevil motorcyclists, darting and weaving between obstacles. Today we'll get there and tomorrow it will all begin.*

He made his way down to the small, smoky kitchen, where he waited with the rest of his family for Cousin Ivor's housekeeper to bring their eggs, toast, sausages and bacon. *She really bangs the plates down on the table. Is that because she doesn't like having to cook a hot breakfast? No, of course not. It's because she's angry with Cousin Ivor for treating her like a servant. Then who can blame her when she shares his bed each night? She's nice-looking, too, while he must be a good ten years older than her.* Julius tried to imagine her days. *She'll be Catholic, as what else would she be in a place like this, so goodness knows how things are between her and her family. If they're even still speaking? And here's Ivor strutting about like the lord of the manor and telling her to get the salt. No wonder that neighbour woman didn't like him.* He glanced around the table. *They're all eyes, naturally. Mother doesn't know what to do with her smile while Claude's trying his damnedest to pretend he hasn't seen a thing. Maude's smirking. Frank's the only one who seems not to have noticed. He's just thinking, yum, tasty eggs and bacon. Now Ivor's telling her to get more milk. You'll pay for all this when we've gone, cousin, I bet.* Julius slipped a sausage onto the floor. *You like a good hot breakfast, don't you, Pazzo?*

The evening before, when they arrived and Ivor saw the state of their car, he suggested they go to a nearby mechanic, whom he praised as 'a good, sound chap', and so, when they had all finished breakfast and loaded the luggage into the Austin, they set off in convoy, with Ivor leading the way in his little Fiat. 'What a charming house-keeper your cousin has,' said Lilian as they drove. 'And very attractive, too.'

I knew she wouldn't be able to resist saying something.

Though she's careful not to say it clearly. It's like she's tap-dancing around a slug.

'She's a good cook, all right,' said Claude with feigned uninterest. 'She knows how to make a proper hot breakfast.'

And you're insisting there's no slug there. Keep the family name whitewashed.

'I'm sure she's good at more than just cooking,' said Maude archly.

Oops. There goes the slug.

'I don't get it?' said Frank.

Oh dear. Now they're all pretending there's no squashed slug after all.

They stopped to wait as a farmer drove his sheep across the road. 'As Ivor spoke so highly of this mechanic,' said Lilian, 'perhaps we should ask if he can replace that awful lamp that the Austrian put on. For that matter he might be able to find some paint that matches better, too.'

Claude was keen. 'Good idea, Pet. It'd be splendid to have the car looking in good fettle for the wedding.'

Absolutely not! Wake up, Predictor. The Other's trying to stop us. 'But I thought we have to be in Rome tonight?' said Julius.

'It wouldn't be the end of the world if we're here for another day,' said Claude. 'In fact, Ivor was rather hoping we might change our minds and stay on.'

Julius' concerns eased when they reached the garage. *This looks even worse than the Innsbruck place.* In the forecourt was a tractor so uniformly rusty that it was impossible to guess what colour it had originally been, together with a battered old truck with poles sticking out from the back. A man was standing on a crate leaning right into the latter's engine, so he looked somehow headless. *That must be the mechanic. I wonder if he'll try and give us parts from the tractor?* Emerging, the mechanic gave a slow stare at the Austin's many injuries. Through Ivor's translation, he told them that it would be impossible to find a replacement lamp. As for the buckled rear end of the car, he would have to remove the back seats and the work would take half the day at least, while even then it would be a poor sort of job, as he didn't have the right paint. Disappointed, Claude agreed that he should restrict himself to the urgent task of fixing the trunk rack. *Just as I hoped. Hurrah! I'm darting and weaving, darting and weaving.*

Within the hour the mechanic had beaten the rack into shape, and welded on a bar where the metal had cracked, so it could support Lilian's trunk, which he tied up with coils of rope to hold it together. Yet Julius' scares were still not quite over. Everyone said their goodbyes to Ivor, who sped away in his Fiat, they climbed into the Austin, Claude put the car into reverse and there was a loud sound of scraping of metal. *The poles sticking out from the truck. I swear he has a kind of talent.*

'It was on my blind side,' said Claude angrily, as if the blame lay with his location in the car. 'And that idiot truck should never have been there.'

Lilian opened her door only to slam it shut again. 'Claude, I swear you're the worst driver in Europe.'

The mechanic's looking at us in wonder.

Frank, who had the window seat that day, climbed out. 'This door still opens all right,' he said. 'It's just a scrape, though it is rather long.' He tried Lilian's door, adding, brightly, 'And this is fine too.'

You've taken on a hopeless task, trying to make the worst driver in Europe look better.

'D'you want me to ask—' Claude began, only to be cut short by Lilian.

'No, I want us to go, and right now, before you hit anything else.'

Thank goodness. Darting and weaving.

'If only we had another driver,' said Lilian as they drove out from the garage. 'You don't know how to drive, do you, Julius?'

You really are desperate. 'No, sorry,' he said. 'Just the motorbike. And I don't have my licence here.' *We're back on the road. Thank you, Predictor!*

As they passed along a wide valley, Claude tried to put a better front on things. 'I'm not saying these little prangs aren't an awful shame, and I am sorry, Pet, of course I am, but these are flesh wounds, nothing more. The car's heart beats strong and she drives fine, absolutely fine.' But his words were undermined moments later. Julius looked ahead through the windscreen and saw the familiar sight of a dark dot surrounded by a halo of beige, and Claude called out, 'Windows shut!' only to be answered by a loud tinkling of glass.

'I didn't do anything,' said Frank anxiously, as the car became filled with dust. 'It just sort of fell out.'

'D'you want me to . . . ?' Claude began.

'No, I don't,' said Lilian icily. 'Just keep going.'

Thank you again, Predictor!

The rest of the journey was breezy and marked by intermittent dust invasions that brought fits of coughing. Frank and Maude grumbled that they couldn't play cards as they might blow away. *Who needs the Slimers when there's so much to see? Those tall thin trees that look a little like green Egyptian obelisks – what are they called? – and little towns perched on top of steep hills. I wonder why they built them up there? To be safe from enemies lurking all around, I suppose. There must've been a lot of enemies.* An odd thought came to him. *Whatever happens, at least I've seen all these things.*

Nobody can make me unsee them now. He brushed away the feeling. *South, south, south. With every mile we drive, we're another mile closer to the Foreign Press Club, and to our victory, Predictor.*

For lunch, rather to Julius' annoyance, they made a small detour, driving up the side of an immense rocky crag to the town of Orvieto, whose narrow lanes Claude negotiated his way through with studied care. *It's too late to impress us with your caution now.* They parked opposite the cathedral. *Look at the facade. I never imagined a church could be so colourful.* Lunch was very good – Julius had pasta with wild boar sauce – but, likeable though the town was, he was more than happy to get back on the road. *South, south, south.*

'I still find it a little hard to believe,' said Maude, as they passed another town crammed onto the summit of a hill. 'In just four days' time, Lou will be a respectable married woman. Just think of it. Mrs Freddy whatever-he's-called. I wonder what the wedding will be like? I imagine Italian ones are quite lavish.'

'The church sounds charming,' said Lilian. 'It's tremendously old, Lou says.'

'I'm sure it's nice enough,' said Claude, 'but I can't help wishing it was happening in a good, plain English church rather than one of these gaudy papal monstrosities, full of statues hysterically waving their arms, and those dreadful babies with wings.'

I'm surprised you're offering an opinion. Are you sure you're forgiven yet?

'I rather like the flying babies,' said Lilian coolly.

As I thought – you're not. I can't believe Mother really loves those cherubs. Unless she thinks they're like her fairies. Now Claude's trying to backtrack.

'I'm not saying there's anything wrong with them, Pet. I just prefer English churches, that's all.'

As the afternoon wore on, the traffic around them grew gradually busier and buildings by the roadside more frequent, till finally Frank let out a shout: 'Look. We must almost be there.' Ahead of them, a small, one-carriage tram was trundling along the road. They overtook it, passed beneath an arch and crossed a narrow bridge.

'This must be old Father Tiber,' said Claude.

I'd expected it to be bigger. Julius glimpsed an athletics track and they began driving down a long straight road beside a tramline, when there was a loud clack, then another. 'Not something else with the car?' asked Lilian, throwing a glance at Claude.

'No, it's them,' said Frank, angrily pointing to a cluster of boys by the tramway. 'They're chucking stones at us.'

They look barely out of nappies they're so small. But they're good shots.

Claude braked sharply and brought the car to a stop. 'How dare they? Just because the car's had a little scrape or two is no excuse for vandalism.'

Frank opened his door. 'I've a good mind to teach them a lesson.'

Good idea. Go and box some toddlers.

But the boys were already scampering away, laughing.

'That would never happen in Germany,' said Maude as they drove on.

Julius felt like singing. *Someone could drop a boulder on the car for all I care. It's done its work. Well done, Austin. You got us here and everything will be all right.*

Claude wound down the window and shouted at passers-by in French till an elderly man, who was walking a very small dog, understood and gave directions. They drove through a park and then into a gate in the city wall. *I wonder how old that is? History never was my strong suit. A thousand years? Two thousand? Five thousand?* They stopped outside the hotel.

'Are you sure this'll be all right?' asked Lilian. 'The places we just passed looked much smarter.'

'It's good value,' Claude told her. 'Italy's so damnably expensive – not like Germany. And there's a garage for the Austin. I wanted to be sure it was safe.'

Quite so – we don't want anything to happen to our beautiful car. Everyone got out and a porter emerged with a trolley for the luggage. *You look so awkward, Claude, even though he's giving you a friendly smile. And the way you hand him the car keys, arm stretched straight and looking away, it's like you're giving farthings to a leper. Let me guess – you're worried he'll laugh at the car. To be honest, he does look like he's struggling to seem as if he hasn't noticed.* For the second time, Julius felt almost a little sorry for his stepfather. *What a life you must have, living each hour desperate to be shown respect, and terrified you won't be. It must be like being in a kind of cage.*

At the reception desk, Claude got out their passports. 'But there are only four here. Where's Julius'? I hope to heaven it isn't back in Venice.'

Damn, I forgot to put it back. 'I have it,' said Julius, opening his suitcase. *I don't care about your suspicious looks.*

'I don't understand,' said Claude accusingly.

'I took it back from the Venice hotel,' said Julius. *Half true.* 'I needed it to change some money.' *And that's a quarter true. Which makes an eighth.* He handed it over. *Claude doesn't believe a word but he doesn't know what to say. As if any of matters now that I'm nearly home and dry.*

The receptionist had a note from Louisa, inviting them to meet her and Frederico for dinner at a restaurant. 'How lovely,' said Lilian. 'We'll just have enough time to change.'

Lou! And I'll finally meet Freddy. The duel begins.

Claude leaned over the desk towards the receptionist. 'I say, I don't suppose you have somebody here who can look after our dog for a few hours?'

'I can call someone,' the receptionist offered.

I need him to help me. 'Surely we can take him along,' said Julius.

'I really don't think that's a good idea,' said Claude. 'I'm sure this is a very smart place.'

'Nobody's minded anywhere else we've been, and he's just a little dog,' said Lilian. 'Of course Pazzo can come.'

Thank you, Predictor. That comes of smashing Mother's car twice in two days, Claude.

Soon afterwards, the family walked out of the hotel, beneath buildings yellowed by the early evening sun. *So these are the famous Spanish Steps. They look like a theatre set. No, a studio set for a song and dance spectacular. A Busby Berkeley. I can just see it. A hundred hoofers lining each side, furiously tapping away, as the leads – he in top hat and tails and she in a flowing dress – swing and leap, all the way down to that little fountain.*

The restaurant was grand, just as Claude had predicted, but Pazzo was allowed inside without a murmur, and they were led to a long, finely laid out table. *Here's Lou. And I'm the one she's making for first. Good old Lou!*

'Hello, Ju. How nice to see you.'

'And you.' *And here's Freddy, the Other's lackey. For some reason I thought he'd be older. He's pretending to be friendly but his smoothness gives him away. I see the real you in your eyes – the shouting bully.*

'I didn't know you had a dog,' said Louisa.

Pazzo stood in front of Frederico, waving his tail. *Thank you, Pazzo, but there's no need – I know all about this one.* 'We found him on the journey here,' Julius shouted to her over the din of excited greetings. 'Actually, Claude ran him over.' *Why are you wagging your tail at Lou?*

'Poor thing. But he looks all right. And he has a most unusual lead.'

Of course. He's just warning me that she's with Freddy. But not for much longer. 'I got him a proper one in Venice, but he didn't like it and chucked it into a canal.'

Louisa broke into peals of laughter.

I thought you'd like that, Lou.

As they took their places, Louisa announced to everyone that she'd had a telegram from Harriet and Harold, who'd been held up in Florence and wouldn't get in till late. 'Which is a shame, but they'll be here for the dinner with Freddy's family tomorrow night, which is the main thing.'

So they won't be able to help me after all. To his own

surprise, Julius wasn't troubled. He felt a sense of strange joy spread through him, in his stomach, his chest, his arms. *I'll do just fine without them, I know I will.*

He found himself seated opposite a thin, pallid priest who explained, in a mild Dublin accent, that he had been instructing Louisa in Catholic rites. 'Poor Father Walsh,' said Louisa with a laugh. 'He's been very patient as he suffers through my ignorance.'

'Which is purest nonsense, as you very well know,' the priest scolded her. 'Louisa's been an excellent student and one of the best I've had the honour to teach.'

Julius let the waiter fill his glass with red – *a sip or two will do me no harm as I'm quite fine now* – and glanced at Louisa's priest. *It's strange, but it's as if I know every thought in your head. It's like I can feel them. They're about the little, plain cell where you sleep. About holy water and benediction. About sitting in a chilly confessional box listening to people's sins, most of them rather dull. They're about impressing your bishop, about praying, and about saving our poor, lost, heathen souls. They're about chastity and not thinking about nakedness. They're about who's in your Catholic club, and who's out. And of course, they're about Jesus, God the Father, the Holy Ghost and Satan.* Julius felt himself smile. *Though what you don't know is that Jesus and the other two, if they're even out there, are all controlled by the Predictor. And the Devil's controlled by the Other. But don't worry, little priest, I won't trouble you with all that. Not tonight.*

'I know he must be tremendously busy,' said Claude at the end of the table. 'But if it were possible, I'd very much like to tell him how much I admire him, and everything that he's achieved. He's given hope to the world in these dark days.'

Who's Claude crawling to Freddy about? Of course – he's trying to get an audience with Mussolini. To make up for Hitler. And so he'll have something to boast about when he gets home. Frank's trying to pretend he's not listening but I can see in his face that he's desperate to go too. The real question is, does Mussolini want to meet Claude?

'You're right, he is very busy,' said Frederico. 'But I'll certainly see what I can do.'

Sounds like the answer's no.

'First, though, it would be my pleasure to show you all my city, if you will allow me. Are you busy tomorrow?'

'Not at all, and that would be most kind, if you have time.'

'Then it's all arranged.'

Julius felt a moment of anxiousness. *Is that to stop me getting to the Foreign Press Club?* A wine bottle hovered above Julius' glass. *Why not? It's tasty.* When he could, he sneaked a glance in his sister's direction, only to find himself confused.

She looks happy enough. And her glances at Freddy the Fascist seem nothing less than adoring. I don't understand. Harriet said . . . Then, though, he noticed how her smile would sometimes falter. *When she thinks nobody's watching her. There it is again. Her mouth drops at the ends and she looks suddenly weary. Thank you, Predictor! No, this shouldn't be too hard at all.*

That night in the hotel, troubled by a conundrum, Julius found it hard to sleep, and he lay restlessly in his bed, hearing distant bells chime each quarter hour. *Too late, too early, too early, too late. I have to go out early so I won't be dragged off on Freddy's tour. But everybody knows that journalists sleep in because they stay up so late drinking. This Manchester Guardian correspondent probably won't get to the foreign correspondent's club till lunchtime at the earliest. But if I'm gone all morning then they'll all wonder where I've got to. They'll think I've gone lunatic again and come searching for me. Damn, damn.* He tossed and turned, trying to see his way to an answer, till finally he was woken by the sound of the door creaking and, opening bleary eyes, he saw Frank walk in wearing a towel, back from the shower. *Now I've overslept. Too early, too late. Predictor, what* . . . But then he saw it had given him an answer without even being asked. *Of course, Pazzo's solved it.* The dog was scratching at the door. 'I'd better take him out,' said Julius, hurriedly dressing. *Thank you, Predictor.*

Just as Harold had promised, the Foreign Press Club was close to the Trevi Fountain, not far from the hotel, and Julius found it with ease. Better again, when he walked inside, he saw a number of journalists were already gathered there, none of whom, to Julius' puzzlement, looked the worse for wear from a late night. When Julius asked for the Rome correspondent of the Manchester Guardian he was met with laughter and a cry of, 'Good luck.' *Damn.* But then it emerged that, though the paper did not have its own representative in the city, there was a stringer who covered stories for them and who, it so happened, was in that morning. *Thank you, Predictor. Darting and weaving.* Julius surprised himself with a notion. *Is this how history happens? Do great events turn on the toss of a coin? Are the lives of millions changed forever because somebody got up early, or late, or lost his balance and fell off his horse?*

Julius was pointed to a prune-faced man who introduced himself as Geoff Stephens. 'And what can I do for you?'

'I have a story for you,' said Julius. 'A really good story.' *Some of the others are looking round. And so you should. This'll be the story of the year, of the decade, the century.*

'Let's go out and get a coffee.'

In a bar around the corner, Julius proudly took the pages

from his pocket and explained about his journey to the wedding, the visit to Dachau and the moment when Joachim had barged into him. *Why is he frowning?*

'The thing is, Germany really isn't my patch,' said Geoff.

'But it's a really huge story, that could . . .' *He's shaking his head.*

'But how d'you know it's so huge? I thought you said you don't understand German?'

It's all going wrong. I can't believe this. I don't understand. There must be a way that can I turn it round. 'Just think of the risk he took giving it to me. Think what would have happened to him if he'd been caught. I know it's important, I just know it. If you'll only have it translated and then send it to the Guardian, I promise you that it'll be a big piece of news.'

'Look, I'm sorry, but I'm not going to pay out to have this translated when there's nothing to say it'll be any good.'

Julius saw a chance. 'I can pay.' *Yes, he's keener now.*

'If you want to—' He rubbed his chin. 'There's someone I know who could take a look if you like, though it'll cost you . . .' He counted the pages and a thoughtful look passed over his face. 'A hundred lire.'

That's not much more than a pound. I thought it'd be more. Thank goodness I changed that money in Venice. 'That's fine.'

Geoff was smiling now. 'All right then. If it does turn

out to be good, like you say, then I'm sure the paper will pay you back, but if not, then I warn you that it'll be your risk. You won't see a penny. Are you happy with that?'

'Certainly I am.' Julius counted out two rust-coloured fifty-lire banknotes. *He thinks I'm a fool, a strange fool, but I don't care in the slightest. You'll see I'm right soon enough, Geoff the Stringer.* 'Can he do it today?'

'Tomorrow morning, I'd say. He's a funny sort of chap. He got out of Germany himself a few months ago and had a bad time of it, by the sounds of things. He's a bit of a vampire and likes to work through the night. But he's translated German bits and bobs for other people at the Press Club, and they've been happy enough.'

'Today would be better.' *Another wary look.*

'I'll see what I can do.'

Julius wrote out his name and his hotel room number in Geoff's notebook and then, with slight reluctance, he handed over Joachim's pages. 'Be sure you don't lose them.'

'I won't, don't you worry.'

'And you'll let me know as soon as you have any news.'

'Of course.'

Walking away, Julius felt a heady lightness, as if an immense weight had been lifted from him. *I've done it. And it wasn't even hard.* He stopped at a butcher's to buy Pazzo a piece of steak. *There's your reward for helping me. Gosh, that went down fast.* Climbing the Spanish Steps, he anticipated trouble – *Claude will kick up a fuss because I was away again* – but when he walked into the hotel dining room, he found the others, surrounded by the remains of breakfast, were smiling and laughing. *Freddy's in his uniform. Very smart and black. Showing your true colours today, aren't you? Still no sign of Harold and Harriet. So much for the great family reunion in Italy – we've only seen them once. But I've done fine without them.*

'They can send someone to collect it this morning, if you like,' said Freddy.

'Perfect,' agreed Claude keenly. 'That'd be quite wonderful.'

Maude had seen Julius' puzzlement. 'Freddy knows of a garage that can fix the Austin,' she explained. 'And it'll cost half what it would in London.'

'This is so kind, Freddy,' said Claude, 'it really is.'

Happy fascists, happy fascists. Aren't you doing well, Freddy, impressing them all? But it's not them you have to worry about.

For his tour of the city, Frederico had a large Fiat car waiting outside the hotel, a uniformed driver behind the wheel. *A chance to study the enemy. And I've always wanted to see Rome. Fountains and churches and temples. This'll be my reward for a job well done.* But, as in Munich, the sightseeing was not as Julius had expected. Their first stop was on a boulevard flanked by high apartment blocks that had a faintly military appearance, with undecorated walls and bleak, square windows. Everyone got out of the Fiat and Frederico made a short speech, recounting how fascism was freeing the Romans from dark, ancient slums, to live in new homes such as these, that were full of air and light.

You're fake, Freddy. I see it, even if none of the others do. It's there in your smooth way of speaking, like an actor performing his lines. Even when you're speechifying about the glories of fascism, you have a little fake smile.

'For our Duce,' Frederico told them, 'the Italian people are like pencil drawings on blank paper, which can be erased and drawn new.' After years of decadent liberal democracy, he recounted, which had reduced Italians to selfish individualists, they were being remade as a collective people, who thought only of their duty to the state. 'A courageous people who will sail across the seas and conquer new lands. A strong people, healthy in their minds and their bodies. The new Italians.'

'Bravo,' said Claude, applauding, as did the others.

Bravo to the man who's having our car fixed at a most reasonable price. Bravo to the man who's taking our twenty-six-year-old daughter off our hands, so he can bully her half to death. Though you won't get the chance, Freddy. I'll see to that. Everybody's clapping, so I suppose I better had too.

'These new Italians,' said Maude. 'Are they anything like the ones we met in that little town a couple of evenings ago?'

Claude and Frank shot her looks.

The mayor whose mistress uses his official car to go shopping? Maude, how could you? Insulting the creed of your not-to-be-half-brother-in-law. Actually, Freddy doesn't look too bothered.

'Revolutions are not completed overnight,' he said patiently. 'They take time and planning. It's no different for your Hitler. And our task is greater. We have to undo half a century of decadent, liberal democratic sickness. Germany has only fifteen years to erase.'

I wonder if it really is possible to remake people, like drawings on a page? It might be nice in a way. Julius remembered the wide windows of his dormitory in the Mid-Wales Hospital. *We had lots of light there, certainly. It streamed in each morning, at least when it wasn't raining. Perhaps whoever built it had the same idea as these fascists?* He remembered Orderly Harris telling him how most patients ended their days on the slab in the hospital mortuary. *If so, it didn't work very well there.*

Back into the car they climbed, to their next stop in the old centre, which was a building site where gangs of workers were chipping away at walls with pickaxes. Frederico explained that it had been an old piazza that was a favourite haunt of foreign painters and writers, and which was being demolished as part of fascism's war against the picturesque.

The picturesque? Good choice – no end of targets in this country. Mother looks appalled. But have no fear, picturesque Italy – you'll be safe soon. Just a few days now.

After lunch they drove to an exhibition of fascism. Attached to the front of the building, which had an old-fashioned, decorated style, were immense fascist columns that were quite out of scale with the rest. Julius tapped one. *Plaster? Or papier mâché? The fascist militiamen standing in front in their uniforms look like they've been hired by a cinema to publicize a new war film.* Walking inside, passing a large cardboard gun, he reached the first room. *Oh hell, Frederico's explaining every picture and every bloodstained martyr's shirt. This is going to take hours.* Julius slipped ahead of the rest, passing photographs of soldiers in trenches, of riots, and a huge map of Italy marked with jagged arrows descending on the capital from all directions. *I think I can guess this one. The March on Rome.* A figure walking ahead of Julius made him start. *Is that Walrus? No, it can't be. I'm sure Walrus was a little taller.*

He walked into a huge, dimly lit room where visitors stood in subdued respect. *I quite like this – very striking. It could be a film set, except that it's much too dark. No film could handle it.* A large curved structure contained strips of faint lights that shone onto a stark, black cross. *What does that mean? 'Father is immortal'? No, no, it'll be something about the immortal fatherland. And that music playing softly in the background must be some fascist anthem. It sounds so sad. I'd have expected it to be lively, like a military march.* He found himself looking at two figures with their backs to him who seemed familiar. *Is that . . . ? But it can't be, surely, not here?* He walked over. *It is.* 'Harriet and Harold. This is a surprise.'

Harriet let out a giggle. 'Oh Gawd, we've been pinched. How very shaming.'

A woman with a group of tiny uniformed children gave a hiss at this disrespectful chatter, and they made their way out into the corridor.

'Don't worry, we haven't jumped ship,' Harriet explained. 'We just came to get our train tickets stamped. You see we get seventy per cent back if we can show we came to the exhibition. A little gift from the fascist state.'

'More for the party's coffers,' said Harold with a grin. 'Money for the cause is money for the cause, no matter where it comes from.'

'So tell me,' asked Harriet, 'have you talked to Lou?'

'Not yet.' *I told you I won't need to now.* 'But you're right about her. She looked miserable at the dinner last night, and I can see he's a bully.'

'Of course I'm right.'

But that's not my real news. Excitedly, Julius told them about his triumph with Geoff the Stringer.

'You paid him in advance?' asked Harriet, looking doubtful.

'I had to. Otherwise he wouldn't have done a thing.'

'Well, let's hope he doesn't just swan off with your lire.'

'He won't,' said Julius, trying to feel confident. *I hope not. Please, Predictor, don't let that happen.*

'Anyway, we'd better beetle off,' said Harriet. 'If we run into all my fascist relatives in here, I'll never hear the end of it. You won't snitch on us, will you?'

'Of course not.'

'Good man. And hurry up and get working on that sister of yours. Try and get her alone at this awful dinner tonight. I'll be watching you.'

As they drove back in the Fiat, Maude complained that the exhibition wasn't half as good as Dachau. 'It was just a lot of photographs. In Dachau you could see things being done.'

'Photographs can inspire, don't forget,' said Frederico. 'Winning even one mind, one heart, that is a victory.'

Perhaps the translation will already be there, waiting for me? I know Geoff the Stringer said tomorrow morning, but when I asked couldn't it be sooner, he didn't say no, he said he'd look into it. Those were his words – I'll look into it. And it shouldn't take that long. Joachim's notes were just six pages, even if he did write over each twice. So it could be there. But when he walked into the foyer and glanced at the rack, there was nothing but the key. Julius tried to slow his racing thoughts. *Geoff said it wouldn't be ready till tomorrow, remember. It doesn't mean anything's wrong. Probably.*

They just had time to dress for dinner, and for Julius to give the dog to the hotel staff. *Sorry, Pazzo. How I wish you could come and help me, but Claude says I absolutely can't take you this time. I hope they make a big fuss of you.* Frederico had sent the Fiat and Julius watched as they drove through narrow roads, then past a fountain – *what are they doing with those turtles? Flipping them over or trying to catch them?* – and, yards later, they came to a stop in front of a high, ancient-looking building. Their driver got out to ring the bell and then a servant emerged and led them into a deep courtyard, with fragments of old reliefs embedded in the walls. *Into the Other's lair. It's huge – a real palace. The Freddies must be loaded. I'm surprised Lou never said anything.*

'A very fine building,' said Claude. 'Most impressive.'

'Yes, quite lovely,' Lilian agreed.

Maude, as ever, was more direct. 'Clever old Lozenge. She has done well, hasn't she?'

Mother and Claude can hardly contain themselves. You're both thinking of the boasting you can do when you get home. I can just imagine it. 'They're Italians, of course, but delightful people and they have the most wonderful palace – yes, it's an actual palace – right in the centre of Rome.' What a surprise you'll have when they lose it all, every ancient brick.

They climbed a broad stone stairway – *you could ride a horse up here* – and were led into an immense room with high windows. *Servants with wine and snacks and a big crowd of Freddies. Those must be his parents. They don't seem very smiley. Does that mean they're with the Other, too? But if they were, then surely they'd be friendlier, just to fool me? Pazzo, this is when I really need you. Unless it's something else completely, and they aren't keen on this wedding. Did they have somebody else lined up for their darling fascist son? An heiress with a castle in Tuscany, rather than the daughter of London suburbanites?*

Harold and Harriet appeared. *Harold's the only one who doesn't look in awe of this place. But then his big pile in Gloucestershire will be twice as grand.* Harriet shot Julius a look. *Yes, yes, I haven't forgotten.* Julius took a second glass of wine and found himself in conversation with a woman who introduced herself as a cousin of Frederico's mother. 'We rode on ponies together when we were little.' She gave Julius a quizzical look. 'So tell me, which are you? The older brother?'

The lunatic older brother who's just been sprung from a mental hospital, that's what you mean. 'That's right.'

240

She glanced round the room. 'And which is your sister who dreams of having tea with Hitler?'

'My half-sister.' Julius pointed out Maude. *She's not very friendly, either. Is her daughter the Tuscan heiress that Freddy was supposed to marry?*

'And the communist one with the communist husband?'

Julius pointed again. 'Harriet and Harold.'

'You English are so strange,' she said, with the faintest of smiles. 'You like so much to dress up. Putting on a play in your drawing room, or going to a fancy-dress party. Or playing at politics and dressing up as Lenin or Hitler.'

Julius was beginning to find her annoying. 'You do your share of dressing up here, too.'

'But here it's different,' she scolded him. 'For you rich English, it's a game. A way to make sure nobody thinks you're dull. And if you lose, nothing terrible will happen, because it doesn't in England. Here we have no choice. We have to dress up, whether we like to or not, and if we lose, we lose everything.'

'I don't see why it's so risky, when everyone here's dressed in the same costume – a black shirt.'

She gave him a quizzical look. 'Don't be so sure you know us. If you live in an old country like this, that has seen so much, then you know it's good to be careful. For example, if an important family . . .'

This family.

'. . . were strongly against a man who then became leader . . .'

Mussolini.

'. . . and enemies could use this against them, then one of them might have to dress up to protect the others.'

'Like Freddy?'

Her look was one of distaste.

For saying what you're really talking about. How gauche of me. I know what you're trying to do. You're trying to make me think he isn't really with the fascists, or Hitler, or the Other, and that he's just looking after his family, but you won't succeed. I know who he is. And then there he was, detached at last from a cluster of people gathered around his parents, and walking alone across the room. 'Sorry,' Julius said to the cousin, 'but there's someone I should talk to.'

'As you like.'

I'll ambush him. I'll catch him out. I'll find a way of saying 'The Other' ten times over. I so enjoyed your tour today as I really felt I was seeing The Other side of Rome. The Other thing I liked . . . Then I'll talk about bad husbands who bully and beat their poor wives. Yes, and I'll tell him how I went to the Foreign Press Club this morning and talked to a stringer for the Manchester Guardian. 'Hello, Freddy.' *The joust begins.*

Frederico looked round in surprise and his mouth broke

into a broad smile. 'Julius – the one I most wanted to talk to here.' He gave Julius a conspiratorial smile. 'I'm sure I shouldn't tell you this, but Louisa is always saying that you're her favourite in the family.'

Fake, fake. You don't fool me. You can't make me like you. Duck and weave, like a boxer. I know just how to knock you off your perch. 'I enjoyed your tour today,' he began. 'It was . . .' He paused, unable to remember the phrase he had planned to say.

'Are you all right?' asked Frederico.

'I'm fine, absolutely fine. As I was saying . . .' The words had slipped away again.

Frederico gave him a concerned look. 'There's something that both Louisa and I wanted to tell you, and that I know we should have said before, but we never found the chance. I think you know that we came over to visit London last Christmas. Louisa so much wanted to . . .' he hesitated, 'come and see you. In Wales.'

Julius felt tears gathering in his eyes. *This is cheating. And we've hardly even started.*

'And I did too, but . . .' Frederico hesitated again.

No, you didn't. It's just another damn lie.

'But we were told that it wasn't the right moment.'

By Claude and my mother. More lies? Perhaps? Probably.

'Afterwards, Louisa wished she hadn't listened to that

advice. She'll tell you herself, I know, but I wanted to say something now. That she was sorry. That we both were.'

Julius willed the tears to stay in his eyes, half born. *I'll show him.* 'I did enjoy your tour today,' he began again, 'as it was wonderful to see the other side of Rome,' but Frederico only smiled.

'I'm so glad.'

What was I going to say next? To make him crumble? But now a pair of double doors had swung open, Julius glimpsed part of a long table crowded with shining cutlery and glasses, and saw that Freddy was gesturing towards the other room.

'I think we'd better go through.'

You probably got the doors to open then on purpose. You gave a secret sign. To save yourself. Well, you're not saved, Freddy. Just you wait and see, I'll win in the end. Tomorrow.

Several hours later, his stomach heavy with all the food he had eaten, Julius climbed out of the Fiat with his family. As he walked into the hotel, his eyes darted to the key rack. *No, still nothing.* 'Nobody left something for me, I suppose? A package, a letter?'

'No, sir, sorry.'

Frank was looking at him. 'What letter?'

'I don't know. I just thought I should check.'

'You're doing that queer thing again, squeezing your hands.'

None of your damn business. 'Hello, Pazzo. Good to see you again.' *He's the only one I can trust. Get a good night's rest, that's what I need.* But, lying in bed, Julius again couldn't sleep. *I'm so damn full.* Plate after plate had appeared and then, just when Julius had been certain the meal was all but finished, a large bowl of pasta arrived before him and he realized that all the other dishes had only been starters. *And then there was another pasta, and after that there was that huge piece of fish and vegetables, and then the pudding, too. It seemed rude not to eat it.* He lay, tossing and turning and listening to the ringing of distant bells. *What if Geoff drops in and leaves the translation, and Freddy has somebody down there waiting to grab it? It wasn't long, just six pages, while Geoff said this man was a real vampire, working through the night, in the dark, so he might finish it at any time. And they don't check properly in these hotels. It was so easy to get Claude and Mother's key in Venice.* The bells rang again. *Is that really another quarter of an hour gone? What if it's down there now?*

Twice, Julius' curiosity became too great and he got up from his bed – 'No, Pazzo, you stay here, I'll be back in a moment' – and slipped downstairs. The first time the night porter was friendly, the second time, less so.

'No letters in the night, signore.'

'But you don't understand, this isn't normal post. It's a private delivery.'

'No letters in the night.'

You don't understand. This package will make the whole world right. 'I just thought I'd check.' Back he went to his room. 'Quiet, Pazzo – don't wake Frank.' The longer he lay awake, the more his fretfulness grew. *What if the Other has a way to stop the translator doing his work? What if it's found a way to stop Geoff the Stringer? Sleep, I need to sleep. Unless you are asleep and you're just dreaming you're awake? Damn, there are the bells again.*

Then he woke with a start and once again it was light. This time Frank was already showered and dressed. 'I swear all you do is snore. I'm going down.'

Julius washed, dressed and made his way down as quickly as he was able. *Still nothing. Damn. He promised it would be there this morning.* He reached the dining room and saw a familiar figure with a comical-looking face, sitting with his family. *He was at the dinner last night. Oh yes – Freddy's brother.*

'Freddy's busy at work,' Lilian explained. 'So Paolo's going to show us round today.'

'First the Pontine Marshes,' Paolo told them, 'that Mussolini made dry to stop the malaria. Then we go to the famous aerodrome where brave Italian airmen fly off to explore all the world.'

'That'll be interesting, eh, Frank?' said Claude.

But this is no good. And the wedding's the day after tomorrow. 'When will we get back?'

'And afterwards we'll see the famous fountains of Villa d'Este in Tivoli,' said Paolo. 'And the Villa of Hadrian. So, I think we return in the early evening.'

'And then we're meeting Aunt Edith and Uncle Walter for dinner,' said Lilian, 'as they get in from Paris this afternoon.'

Julius took a bite from a cornetto, then another and another, so his mouth was full. *They're looking at you. Slow down. Perhaps it's all fine? Perhaps Geoff has already sent it to the Manchester Guardian? But I can't leave it to chance. Do I make an excuse? But what?* His mind felt blank, empty and useless. *Now they're getting ready to leave. Predictor . . .*

'Do you need to go . . . ?' said Claude.

'No, I'm fine,' said Lilian.

'But sometimes when we get out onto the road . . .'

'I said I'm fine,' said Lilian sharply.

They walked outside. *The driver's seen us and he's bringing over the car. If I get in, then everything in the whole world will go wrong, but how can I not?* He thought of a spy picture he'd seen once, where the hero had escaped pursuers by climbing into the back of a taxi and then slipping out from the door on the far side. *But even if I get there first, I'll have to shut the door and stop them getting in, so that won't work. And anyway, they're sure to see me climbing out, unless I crouch down very low, and even then . . .*

'That piece of string looks so absurd,' said Claude. 'He'll have to stay in the car when we tour round today. I'm not having him make us look ridiculous.'

That could do. 'You know what, I'll go and get him a proper lead now.'

Claude rolled his eyes. 'For goodness' sake, man, I didn't mean this very moment.'

'But I want to, so Pazzo will look nice. And besides, I don't really feel like seeing all of these places. I'm a bit tired, you see, and I'd rather stay here. And anyway, I need to take Pazzo for his walk.' *He's frowning.*

'I'm not sure that's a good idea, Julius.'

They can't stop me. It's not as if I need their permission. 'And I'd like to take some pictures.' *Sound like you've made up your mind and that's that.* 'So I'll see you all when you get back, all right? For dinner with Aunt Edith and Uncle Walter. Don't worry, I won't be late, I promise.' He glanced down. 'Come on, Pazzo.' *Is Claude going to say something? He looks like he might.*

'Oh, just let him go,' said Maude.

'Bye then.' Julius walked away and heard somebody say goodbye in return. *Thank you, Predictor.* Down the hill he hurried to the Press Club.

'Geoff? I haven't seen him in today.'

Damn. 'D'you know where he lives?' *I'm only trying to do something important and good. Why didn't I get his address yesterday? Fool, fool. The world can change on a flip of a coin, the flip of a coin, the flip of a coin.* 'He's had something translated for me, you see. Into German – no, no, from German into English. I had his address but I must have lost it.' *There's no harm in a little lie to save the world. A quarter lie, a sixteenth.*

The journalist turned and shouted back into the room. 'Does anyone know Geoff's address?'

Somebody did, and Julius had him write it down on a scrap of paper. 'It's safer. I don't know how to pronounce a word of Italian.' Julius gave an awkward laugh. *Thank you, Predictor.* 'Come on, Pazzo.' He hurried out, waving the scrap of paper to passers-by as he went, asking them, 'Excuse me, but d'you happen to know where this place is?' He made his way across a large, round-shaped square in the centre of which was a fountain with an Egyptian obelisk, and four lions spitting out jets of water, then he strode out through a gate in the city wall. *I remember this – we came from up there when we first arrived. Yes, this is the beginning of the tramline where the toddlers threw stones at the car.* He counted the street numbers until he found the right one. *Damn – so many buzzers, and I only remember his first name. It just says Geoff on this piece of paper. I should've asked for the flat number.* He saw an English surname and pressed.

'It's Julius.'

'Oh, hello.' The faint, gramophone-like voice sounded faintly displeased. 'You'd better come up. Fourth floor.'

Emerging from the lift, Julius glimpsed Geoff leaning out of an apartment doorway, dressed in pyjamas and a worn-looking dressing gown. *So I was right about the late night whisky and rum – you just don't do it every night.* As Julius stepped closer, he heard, through the doorway behind Geoff, the sound of an Italian voice speaking on the radio, also a woman cooing and a tiny child's laughter. Geoff gave Julius a smile. 'Beware of small decisions, my friend. And to think I only came here to sell vacuum cleaners.'

As if it matters. As if I care. Can't you see, you're being slow when you need to be fast? 'Did you get the translation?'

Geoff held out a sheaf of papers. 'The original's here too. He turned up just now. I was about to drop it off at your hotel.'

No you weren't, you're in your pyjamas. But it doesn't matter, not a fig, not a jot, not an iota, all that matters is that

I finally have it. Julius caught a glimpse of words: 'Very often the guards . . .'

'So you'll send it to the Manchester Guardian? You'll . . .' Julius tried to remember the phrase Harold had used. 'You'll send it on a wire or by telephone or something, so they can put it in the paper tomorrow?'

Geoff shook his head. 'Not exactly. I'll pop my copy in the post. I had him do two. I did a bit of checking yesterday, you see, and it turns out they ran a piece on Dachau just a few weeks ago, while as far as I can see there's nothing really new in here. So there's no point running up bills using the blower.'

Julius felt his head was spinning. *Impossible. It can't be.*

Geoff had seen Julius' face fall and misunderstood. 'Sorry, Julius. I wish I could pay you back the hundred lire, but this just isn't an earner. And I did warn you.'

As if I care about the money. It makes no sense, no sense at all. 'You read it through carefully?'

'Of course.'

'Then you must've seen how important it is?' *Now he's looking uneasy.*

'Take a look yourself,' said Geoff, handing over the pages. 'This copy's yours. You've paid for it.'

He's holding it out to me at arm's length, keeping his distance. Julius flipped through, glancing at lines: 'every

evening at six . . . beaten to death . . . Gerhart and Franz . . .
the guards are rewarded . . . cleaning faeces from the latrines
with their fingers . . .'

'But this can't be right. I just know it.'

'Julius, I've done everything I can.'

'You don't understand. This will bring down the Nazis,
and Mussolini, too. I know it will.' *He's got that look.*

'I think I'd better go in and give the wife a hand,' said
Geoff, stepping back into the doorway. 'Washing-up and
all the rest. But good to meet you, Julius, and very best of
luck with it all.'

He's going to . . . 'Stop, wait. You've got this all wrong.'
Julius reached out to grab the edge of the door and in that
one instant, Geoff's polite friendliness vanished and, his
eyes staring, angry and scared both together, he slammed
the door shut.

'I don't know what's wrong with you,' he called out, his
voice muffled through the wood. 'But leave me be, d'you
hear? Or I warn you, I'll call the police. I will.' A key turned
in the lock.

Then there was quiet. Julius stood on the empty landing,
listening to the muffled murmurs of the Italian radio voices.
I should have explained it all better. Then he'd understand.
Should I try again? He stared at the notes in his hand. *What*
if the message is hidden in some kind of code? He flipped

through the pages and then realized. *But that won't be in the translation, as it would only work in the original.* He turned the pages over and stared at Joachim's notes, catching sight of the drawing of the bird on the wire. *Does that mean something? But what? No, there's nothing here that I can understand.*

All of a sudden Julius felt blocked, thwarted in every way, so there was nothing to do, nothing to want or need, no purpose remaining. He leaned back against the wall next to Geoff's door. *Was I wrong about everything?* He had a feeling of being smothered. *Or has the Other been cleverer than I thought? For all I know, the translator could've been working for him all along, and he could have deliberately left out the important part of the notes? That would explain why Geoff didn't see how much this matters. He said the translator was like a vampire, working in the dark.* The word hung in the racing patter of his mind. *A vampire, a vampire, working in the dark.*

Julius slumped to the floor and hardly noticed as Pazzo trotted onto his lap and reached up to lick his chin. An elderly couple, both carrying bags of groceries, walked by, casting Julius glances, and hurried to open their door. *As if it matters what went wrong or who did it. The fact is, it's all too late now. The wedding's in two days. Geoff would've had to get it to the paper this morning so they could print it tomorrow. I can't do anything now. All for nothing, all for nothing. The Other won after all.*

Julius heard a door open and watched as a family walked by, with two small children who glanced at him with wide, puzzled eyes. Pazzo growled at them. *I should get up, go somewhere. But I feel like staying here.* It was as if there was a kind of correctness in staying perfectly still, so he could feel that no part of him was moving, aside from the faint shifting of his chest as he breathed. *And that's not much. It's almost still, too.* He heard a key turn in the lock and the door open for a moment, then slam shut before the key turned again. *Geoff. Not worth turning my head to see.*

Then a thought came from somewhere. *But you got here. You can still do what you were going to do.* What the thought offered – a course of action, something like hope – bothered Julius, and seemed somehow distasteful, so he tried to bat it away, but it hovered obstinately before him. *Don't give up. The Predictor's still at your side, helping you.* 'It's too late,' he murmured in what was barely a sound, just the moving of his tongue with hardly a breath exhaled. *No it's not. You owe this to Louisa. And you promised Harriet.* Julius tried to shut out the thought, and pondered blocking his ears. 'As if that would help.' *Come on, get up. You can't just slump here.* 'Can't you just leave me be?' said Julius, but then, to his own surprise, he found himself rising to his feet. 'All right, all right.'

Slow as an invalid, he made his way to the lift, only to hear it whirring, busy. *As if it matters, as if I care.* He started down the stairs, and the movement of his legs seemed slowly to change something in him. *I suppose it might work? Worth a try?* Out he walked into the Via Flaminia, blinking in the bright sunlight. *This is stupid. I don't even know where it is.* He stopped, half blocking the pavement, so people edged past him, but then the thought came back. *Come on now. What would you do in London?* 'Ask a cabbie. They always know.' He turned towards the traffic and, as it happened, a taxi was approaching, and when Julius waved, the driver slowed and veered towards him.

It turned out that Rome cabbies were not like London ones. The driver, who spoke only Italian, and was mystified by Julius' request, began driving through the city, urging Julius to lean out of his window and call out, to anyone who looked like they might understand English. Finally, after Julius had repeated 'British Embassy' a dozen times, a reply came back, 'Ambasciata Brittanica', and the process began all over again, as the driver asked where it was.

Julius was surprised by a jolt of hope. *We're on our way.* Pazzo reached up and licked his nose. The cab climbed up to a sloping, open square with two statues of men and rearing horses, and then drove along a long, narrow road, straight as a ruler, till it came to a stop beside the embassy.

'I wonder if I could speak to Louisa Sewell. I'm her brother.'

And moments later, there she was, giving him an uncertain smile. 'Hello, Ju. Everything all right? You look like you're all in.'

'Everything's fine, absolutely fine.' Julius realized, with a slight start, that until this moment he'd given no thought as to how he might approach the conversation. *Delicate, delicate, that's what it is.* 'There's something I want to talk about, Lou. Something quite important. D'you think they'd mind if we go and get a coffee?'

'If we're quick. You'd never guess I'm getting married in two days, as they're still throwing a ton of work my way. I have a whole report to type up by four.' She pointed. 'There's a place just down here.'

No use beating round the bush. Just take a leap, jump in, never mind if the water's chilly. Harriet said it would be easy, remember. 'The thing is, Lou, I know you don't really want to marry Freddy, and I've come here to tell you, don't. You absolutely mustn't. And certainly not just because you think everybody expects you to.'

Louisa had stopped and was standing on the pavement, staring at him. 'What?'

She'll see in a moment. Predictor, what will make her understand? 'At the dinner last night, I saw how glum and low you looked. You'd seem cheerful enough but then your mouth would sort of droop down at the ends so I could see it was all an act. And it was the same at the restaurant the night before, just the same.' *Oh hell, she's crying.*

She stared at him with wide, tearful eyes. 'I can't believe you're saying this. Freddy's everything to me. I mean, how dare you?'

Tell her about Harriet? The Other? The Predictor . . . ? 'But, Lou . . .'

'If I looked unhappy last night, it was only because I don't feel easy around Freddy's parents. They've never been . . .'

I know all that. The Tuscan heiress. He interrupted her, raising his voice to stop her talking. 'Can't you see, I'm only trying to help you. You just can't do this. He's a fascist and an awful bully and he'll . . .'

'Stop.' The word came out shrill, halting him. Louisa bowed her head. 'This is all my fault. I should have listened to Claude. I should never have told him to take you out of that place and bring you here.'

Julius had the strangest feeling, as if he could see himself from one of the high windows of the buildings above: a skinny figure with gingery hair sticking up from his head, standing by the side of a long, straight road, cars driving slowly by. He felt like his body was delicate and fragile, with no covering to protect it. Into his thoughts, unasked, came the feel of the padding in the little room in the Mid-Wales, where they threw him that time when they put him in the monkey suit: the smells of institutional soap, disinfectant and tea, of old clothes and jungle juice: and the sounds in the ward at night, murmured phrases repeated over and over like prayers, sudden shouts or screams. *Predictor?* Julius had a new sensation, not that it was refusing to answer him, but that it was gone, vanished, and in its place was now an empty void. *The Other's killed it.*

'I'd better find someone to take you back to your hotel,' said Louisa.

Everything's gone wrong. It's all fallen apart. Julius found himself thinking, for some reason, of the fascist militiamen's office in the town near Cousin Ivor's house, and the man who Julius had glimpsed in the chair, crying as he sat in his soiled trousers. *But not everything, not yet. Yes, it's not too late. I can thwart the Other even now if I have the will.* He felt a kind of determination that, despite everything else, was pleasing to him. *Get her to leave you be.* 'It's all right, I can find my own way back.'

'You're sure?'

'Quite sure. I'll be fine, honestly.' He began walking away.

'Julius,' his sister shouted out.

Don't let her stop you. 'Sorry about all this,' he called back to her. 'I'll see you at dinner tonight with Aunt Edith.' *Now don't look back.* After a hundred yards he did and saw she was still standing in the same spot, but then she finally turned away. *A taxi? Why bother? First things first.* 'I'll take you back to the hotel, Pazzo.' He reached a crossroads, noisy with cars, with cramped fountains set into the corner of each building and, looking to the right, he felt a kind of dry, mechanical satisfaction. *That's the obelisk above the Spanish Steps. I always did have a good sense of direction.*

Minutes later he walked into the hotel foyer. 'Can someone here look after my dog?'

'For how long?'

They didn't mind last night. 'Just a few hours. My family will be back later this afternoon.'

'I must ask.'

'Thank you.' Julius embraced the animal, a sinewy thing that pushed at him with its legs and licked his face. 'I'm sorry, Pazzo, I really am. I hope they look after you nicely.' It was only then that he realized that someone was standing beside him.

'Signor Sewell?'

For a moment Julius' sense of recognition deserted him as he looked, confused, into a face he knew but could made no sense of in this place. *Walrus? What are you doing here?*

'I need you please to come with me.'

The Other's trying to stop me. Show him you know, that you're not scared. 'You were following me in Venice.'

Walrus frowned. 'Not you. Signora Harriet and signor Harold. Colonel di Marco asks that you come with me.'

Colonel di Marco? That's Freddy. So it's just as I thought and I was right all along. Walrus is with the Other and Freddy is too. 'Sorry,' said Julius, 'but I have something I need to do.'

'But you must come,' the other man insisted. 'Something has happened. Your sister Harriet and signor Harold met a man who is being watched, a communist, and they were all arrested – not by us, but by another agency.'

Another trick, Walrus, but I'm not fooled. 'I'm sorry, but I really can't help you.'

'Signor Sewell, you don't understand. Colonel di Marco called the other agency and managed to get signor Harold and signora Harriet free, but they wouldn't go and stayed outside the police station, shouting that the communist must be freed too, so they've been arrested again. Now they're demanding to see the British Ambassador.'

Just like Claude.

'But this is dangerous for Colonel di Marco. He asks you

please to talk to your sister and make her stop this. He says you are the one she'll listen to.'

No you don't. 'I'm very sorry, but I really do need to go.' With that, Julius all but threw Pazzo into the arms of the receptionist and, feeling Walrus clutch his arm, pulled it free, turned and dashed out of the hotel. *The Other's a fool to send Walrus. He's far too old and fat.* Julius ran across the street, just dodging a car, and then onwards, down the Spanish Steps, two at a time, almost knocking into a couple of elderly tourists. Reaching the fountain at the bottom he darted into a long, straight road. *Is this the quickest way? It feels like it's down, so it must be right. Yes, we came along here yesterday when we drove home.* He hurried past shops and restaurants until, just as he'd hoped, *there it is up ahead. The embankment.* He sped across the road, hearing car horns ring out and then, suddenly as it seemed, found himself on the bridge, with people turning to see as he ran by. *Slow down. Look like you're just walking along. This should be far enough. That man's staring.* He let himself glance back. *Poor Walrus is still on the other side of the road, huffing and puffing.*

For some reason he thought of his watch. *It's not waterproof. No use in wrecking it.* He took it off only to surprise himself by reaching his arm back and flinging it with all his strength into the void. *That was stupid. Now that man's coming towards me.* Julius heard shouts, didn't look round, made a run for the parapet and got one knee on top, only to feel someone grab his foot. He tried to kick himself free but instead felt his other leg seized. Now he felt himself being dragged back, so he fell, cool stone pressing into his belly. *Damn you, damn you, whoever you are. This is none of your business.* Longingly, he glimpsed dark green water below, but then it was gone, he was tugged backwards, his elbows struck the pavement and he found himself pinned to the ground, shouts all around him. *Someone's sitting on me.* Though he tried to roll over and throw them off, it was no use, and then he felt his arms yanked back and heard a click. *Cuffed. Walrus must have found some police. Damn, damn. I'd have been all right if it hadn't been for that stupid watch. So the Other's won. Won everything.* His eyes wanted to fill with tears. *No, none of that.* But they came anyway.

Finally he felt himself being pulled up from the ground. He quite expected to see a windowless van, like the ones that had taken him to Ticehurst all that time ago, and then to the Mid-Wales – *it'll be a very long drive this time* – but instead he found himself being frogmarched to a small police car, where he was wedged into the back seat, a policeman on one side of him and Walrus on the other. *As if I'd try and jump out.*

'Mister Julius . . .'

Sorry, Walrus. You look scared. Who are we waiting for, I

wonder? Nazis? The Other? But his sense of the Other felt fainter now, like steam vanishing into air. *Oh hell, it's them.* Louisa and Frederico were running along the bridge towards him. *Damn, damn.*

'I'm so sorry,' Louisa called out, still yards away. 'Julius, forgive me.'

If only they'd all leave me alone.

'I won't let them take you back to that place.'

Is she with the Other? But the question seemed old now and he pushed it away.

She reached into the car, past Walrus, and embraced him, pressing her tear-wet face against his, and holding his head with her hands. 'I'll help you, Julius, I will. Do you hear me?'

He did.

Eight

Ten years later, early on a bright June morning, four figures in army uniforms – two with stills cameras round their necks, and a third (Julius) holding a cine-camera – climbed into a jeep and set out towards Rome. Knowing that the main route would be filled with marching soldiers and slow-moving vehicles, the commanding officer had decided they should take a back road that ran parallel to the coast. Just as he had hoped, it proved all but deserted, and for several hours they kept up a sedate pace, the four of them keeping their eyes trained on the trail ahead, watching for landmines. But then in the early afternoon Julius glimpsed something on a rise in the ground up ahead – a straight line breaking the horizon – and at the very same moment as he shouted out a warning, he heard a sound that had become very familiar to him during the past two years: the boom of a German 88 gun. The driver slammed on the brakes, a shell burst a hundred yards before them and they sped back in reverse. After a night in a half-ruined farmhouse just out of range of the 88, they woke at dawn, saw the gun had vanished and, chewing down ration biscuits, they set out onto the road once again.

Hang on, Lou. I'll get to you. I hope. If you're there. Reaching into the pocket of his army jacket, Julius felt a tiny, cool sphere, and he pulled out a glass marble with a green swirl in its centre. He had found it a year before, on the floor of an abandoned café on the coast of Tunisia where he had slept for a few nights, and for some reason he had kept it. He held it over the side of the jeep. *If I drop this, will Lou and Freddy be all right?*

Into his thoughts came Dr Zannoni, sitting in his studio in Rome, books lining the walls, as he watched Julius through his small, round glasses. 'You know better than this, Julius. What do I always tell you? What do you need to ask yourself?'

Where's the evidence?

'And?'

There's none. With a faint feeling of disappointment, Julius brought the marble back towards his pocket. *But it's not just me, Dr Zannoni. What about all the soldiers I've seen before a battle, twisting handkerchiefs between their fingers, or rubbing a special coin, or mumbling a lucky phrase, or making a prayer. How is this any different?*

'I never said it was only you. Don't worry about them. Just worry about yourself.'

All right, Doctor. But then Julius again held the marble over the side of the jeep. *Not because I think it'll help Lou, but because I feel like doing it.* He let the marble fall and watched it bounce, catching the glint of the sun before it vanished into the dust.

An hour after they set out, they reached a small town, seemingly deserted. The driver slowed the jeep to walking pace and Julius and the other three each took a rifle from the rear of the vehicle. Julius saw a face at a second-floor window glance out at them and then vanish.

'They don't seem very friendly,' Julius murmured.

The reason became apparent a moment later. A man peered at them through a doorway, peered again and then broke into a shout. 'Americani!'

They thought we were Germans.

First a few, then a rush of people emerged from the buildings and in an instant the four in the jeep were brought to a halt in the middle of the street, as they were cheered, embraced and kissed. Julius freed himself from the outstretched arms, climbed on his seat to get a clear view and took a few shots while the other two clicked away with their stills cameras. 'That'll do,' said the commanding officer. 'Keep it for the main show.'

They didn't have long to wait. Another hour and they were in Rome, driving down a wide boulevard amid a slow-moving procession of marching soldiers and military vehicles, as a crowd cheered and reached out with flowers and bottles of wine. *The apartment blocks look just like the ones Freddy said would transform Italians with sunlight. It seems like they weren't blank sheets of paper after all. Everyone looks so thin and hungry here. Almost as bad as in Naples.*

Julius' eye was caught by a commotion at the entrance of one of the buildings. A middle-aged couple was being jostled into the street. The man had a black eye and both looked scared.

His commanding officer had seen. 'Make sure you get a shot of those two quislings.'

Julius raised the cine-camera. *Don't let that be Lou and Freddy. Please.*

A few hours later, by which time Julius had canned a good few yards of film, his commanding officer told him that he could go. 'But make sure you're not late. You have the address of our HQ?'

'Yes, sir.'

Julius walked into the crowd, and from his top pocket he took a tiny package. He carefully unwrapped the oilskin that had protected it from Sahara sand and two Mediterranean landings, and took out a small address book. He showed it to a man in a crumpled hat, trying to pronounce the street name, and soon found himself surrounded by a small group of helpers, who pointed him down a street with tram rails. *Wait a minute – I think I remember this. If I'm right then it's not far at all. Down that narrow road. Yes, there's the fountain with the turtles. Are they flipping or catching them? And there's the house.*

Running now, he reached the door, rang the bell and waited. *Perhaps it doesn't work.* He knocked on the wood, then thumped at it with his fist. 'Lou, I'm here, Lou,' he called as loudly as he could. *It doesn't mean that something awful's happened. They could have just gone away somewhere safer. Though I can't think where. Or they could just be out watching the soldiers marching in.* He began walking away, trying to clear his head and think what he should do next, when he heard wood creaking from behind him, and glancing back, he saw a shutter open and a face peer out. *It doesn't look like her. Is someone else living here?* 'Lou?'

For a moment she stared at him, confused. 'Ju, is that you?' She let out a delighted shriek, vanished from the window and moments later the door swung open and they embraced.

Thank heavens, thank heavens, thank heavens. She looks so thin. I hardly recognize her. To his confusion, Julius found he felt angry. 'I was so worried. I thought I'd find you hanging from a lamp post. Because of Freddy.'

She laughed. 'Don't be silly. That's only the ones who

268

threw in their lot with the Germans. Freddy joined the anti-fascists a year ago, when Mussolini fell and everybody did.' He was out, she explained, making contact with the Allied top brass.

Freddy jumped just in time, like Claude. I know he's not a bad man, Lou adores him, he was very kind to me, and he only joined the fascists to protect his family, but I'm still not sure I like him very much.

They began making their way up the grand stairway. 'You can't think what it's been like since the Germans came,' said Louisa. She told him how she and Freddy had hidden dozens of people in the house: Italian soldiers, Jews and Allied airmen. 'At one point we had a real American spy with a radio. We dreaded hearing a rap on the door in the night. I know people who it happened to.'

They reached the sitting room. *Maria and Ludovico.* Ludovico had been little more than a baby when Julius had last seen him, before the war, and Maria wasn't yet born. *You both seem as starved as your poor mother.* For a moment they looked at Julius with wary amazement, then they ran forward to embrace him. Julius put down his cine-camera and opened his kitbag. 'I have something for you.' He brought out tins of bully beef, beans, Spam, steak, soup, sausages, and some chocolate. *Look at their eyes. Even poor Lou can't stop staring.*

'Oh God, Ju, you can't think how welcome this is. We've had hardly anything but a few bits of pasta and greens for weeks. D'you mind if I open one or two now? I can't heat them, I'm afraid, as there's no gas.'

For a time hardly a word was said, as Louisa and her children concentrated only on eating. Finally Louisa sat back in her chair and looked at Julius with something approaching calm. 'It's so strange to see you in a uniform. I never thought you'd be a soldier.'

If the Film and Photographic Unit counts as soldiering. Though we've lost some good men. I've got some scars myself, from Alamein and the Salerno landing. You have to be in the thick of it to get a decent shot.

Louisa was hungry for news of the family. 'All I've had for the last four years are tiny Red Cross letters from Ma that didn't say a thing.'

'They're all fine as far as I know. Thriving, actually.' *Because they jumped just in time.* Julius told her how Claude had a good job at the Ministry of Food with his own government car and driver. 'Frank's a captain in the Guards, somewhere out here in Italy. He's quite the war hero.' Maude still spent all her time going to the strange little baptist church she had joined. Harold was in the RAF, training pilots in Cambridgeshire, and Harriet was serving on an ack-ack battery in Tooting, shooting at German night bombers, and of course writing endless pieces for the Daily Worker. 'And Mother's a secretary for a charity, getting people to knit pullovers for the Merchant Navy. Pazzo's still driving her wild. The last I heard, he burrowed under the fence into the Scriveners' garden.'

Louisa half closed her eyes. 'Not their pedigree spaniel?'

'Yes, she had a very un-pedigree litter. The Scriveners threatened to sue.' *Your laugh sounds faint, like there's no air in you. You always had such a strong laugh. But it'll come back, I'm sure.*

Louisa sat forward. 'And you?'

Julius blinked. 'Not bad, I suppose. I still keep having to ask myself, is this real? And I often think about Dr Zannoni. He was the only one who made any real sense. Is he . . . ?'

'I saw him on the street just a few weeks ago, looking a bit ragged like everybody here does. But he seemed all right.'

'Thank goodness. I'll go and see him if I get the chance. I'd like to thank him.'

Louisa reached out for his hand. 'You've done well, Ju, you really have.'

I suppose I haven't done so badly. I've shot a few good pictures – more poor ones, but that's always the way – and now I've filmed a war. No, I've not done too badly at all. 'It never quite goes away and I don't suppose it ever will. But it can be managed. So far, anyway.' He glanced at his watch. 'Now I'd better get going, as I have to find our new HQ. I don't want them to think I've gone AWOL. I'll try and come and see you again tomorrow with some more tins.' He got to his feet, only to stop. 'Oh, I have one last piece of news. It just goes to show how good things can come from the most unlikely places. I got a letter the other day and you'll never guess who it was from.'

Louisa looked blank. 'That girl you liked years ago?'

'Linda? No. I never saw her again. She left the studio. It was Joachim Holt.' *She looks blank.* 'The one who slipped those notes in my pocket in Dachau.' *Now she remembers, just about.* 'He said he's been trying to find me for years. He wrote to the Manchester Guardian but all they had was the name of the stringer I found here, and he'd gone to live in Australia. But Joachim tracked me down in the end, and . . .' From his pocket Julius took a battered envelope.

'What did he want?' asked Louisa.

'To thank me. It turned out someone at the Manchester Guardian saw his notes and helped get him out of Dachau. Holt's living in Devon with his family. He's a painter, and from what I can make out, rather a good one. So I may not have got rid of Hitler and Mussolini and saved the world, but at least I helped someone.'

It was sunset when Julius left the house. *This city's so*

beautiful, even now, in the middle of a war. The streets, which had been so crowded, were quiet. *Is there a curfew? Or do people go home from habit?* He heard classical music – *Beethoven?* – and, glancing up, he saw, through an upstairs window, an elderly couple arm in arm, slowly dancing. *That would be a nice shot if I had a tripod and a distance lens. Though you really need to hear the music, too. Now which way is this HQ?* He walked and walked until, realizing he was lost, he called out to a man wobbling past on a bicycle, who pointed down the road he had just come. *I must have gone right by it.* Retracing his steps, he passed three drunken soldiers shouting up at a window, 'Signora, signora.' *Leave her be, whoever she is.* He found himself facing marble figures and a rearing horse, just visible in the last dusk light. *I remember this. The Trevi Fountain. It's better with water flowing.*

He heard a faint scratching sound and, looking round, he saw a man and woman were ripping paper from a large black-and-white poster of fasces and a swastika, side by side. It was well attached and the couple were only able to tear off smallish strips. Then, as Julius walked nearer, two men emerged from a side alley and, out of nowhere, a sharp argument broke out. A shape caught the dusk light. *He's got a pistol.* 'Hey!' Julius shouted out. *Very clever when all I have is a cine-camera.* But the sight of an

Allied uniform was enough and the two with the gun flitted away.

The couple who had been ripping at the poster turned to him. 'Grazie, grazie.' They pointed in the direction where the others had fled. 'Fascisti.' They looked as shocked as Julius was. 'But why?' said the girl, disbelieving. 'All is finished now.'

It's true, it makes no sense. But then I suppose you can't expect everything to vanish as easily as that. It'll never quite go away, probably. It'll be something that has to be managed. Julius shook hands with the couple and walked on.

Acknowledgements

I would like to thank Frédérique Matras and Andrew Nadeau for their help with the French dialogue, Reinard Uhimann for his help with the German, and Cymdeithas yr Iaith for their kind help with the Welsh.

I would also like to thank my wife Shannon and our friend Ana Paula Lloyd for their wise advice. And as ever, I would like to thank my agent Georgia Garrett, and also Will Atkinson and everyone at Atlantic Books.